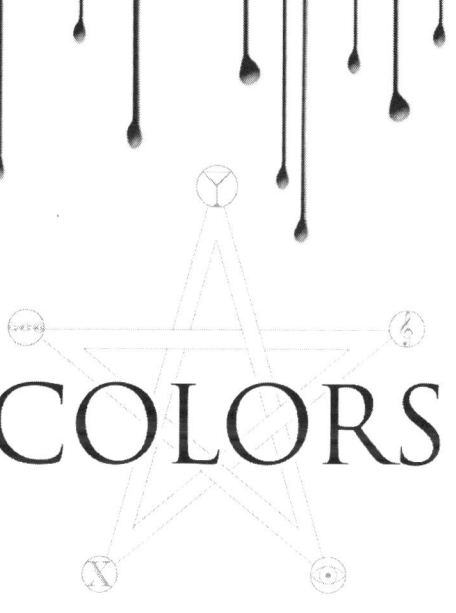

COLORS

Olivia Arndt

Copyright © 2020 by Olivia Arndt

All rights reserved. No part of this publication may be reproduced, distributed, or transmitted in any form or by any means, including photocopying, recording, or other electronic or mechanical methods, without the prior written permission of the publisher, except in the case of brief quotations embodied in critical reviews and certain other noncommercial uses permitted by copyright law.

Printed in the United States of America

Dedicated to mom,

Thanks for always believing in me!

★ hugs ★

Chapter One

As the years flew by, the colors darkened. That was my first memory. I had only been six.

My parents started with bright, fluorescent clouds above their heads, casting beams of sunlight across everything around them. Those clouds had been my lifeline for many years, no matter what happened, what went wrong, they would always make even the darkest days brighter. Then everything changed. Their clouds began to turn into dark, colorless shades of blue, and their moods were no different. They began to fight and no longer sang the song they had once shared. My brother had become the only other light in my life, a small reminder of how it used to be.

One evening, when we were all eating dinner, it suddenly got really quiet. My parents had stopped talking, and my brother was barely eating. I decided to break the silence.

"So," I looked from my parents to Hyperion. "How was everyone's days today?" I piped up. My eyes went to the blue haze above their heads; only my brother's cloud was still yellow.

"Great, sweetie," my dad mumbled through gritted teeth.

"Fine." My mom sighed, setting her plate down. They shared a look that I didn't quite understand.

"Pretty good." My brother smiled at me in between bites of his chicken. "How was yours?"

"Amazing!" I finished my food and jumped out of my chair. "Can I be excused?"

"May," my brother mumbled under his breath. "May I."

"Sure, sweetie." My dad stood up and thrust his plate at my mom. She glared at him but remained silent.

I thought nothing of it and skipped upstairs. As soon as I shut my door behind me, screaming sounded from downstairs. I didn't know what was going on, and I was about to check when Hyperion came rushing into my room.

"What's going on?" I tried to catch a glimpse of what was happening behind him, but he quickly shut the door again.

"Nothing, Tess." He gently led me over to my bed and pulled out my toy elephant, Sprinkles. "Here, let's play with Sprinkles."

"But...well, okay!" I smiled as he pulled out Mr. Bananas, the stuffed monkey. We sat there and played stuffed animals for hours, ignoring everything around us. Eventually, the yelling stopped, and in a matter of seconds, my mother was upstairs muttering comforting words to us.

"What happened?" My brother squeaked, trembling. "Where is dad?"

My mother ignored his question and continued cradling me in her arms. "It's going to be okay."

"Okay," I smiled up at her, but it soon faded as I took in the deep blue hue of her cloud. It was darker than it had ever been before. "Mama?"

"Yes, Tess?" She kissed my forehead and stroked my hair away from my face.

"Never mind…" I looked at her dark cloud sadly. "Can you…can you sing me your song?"

She hesitated for a second, a strange look crossing her face. "Okay." She took a deep breath and began softly singing a sweet melody. One only my father and her knew.

When a child is born, they have a single melody that is sung to them called a soul song; no one else knows the song except for one other person. That person is your soulmate. It's said that when your soulmate dies or when you two break apart, you can never love again. You also cannot marry again, even if you wanted to. Once it was over, that was it, no more love, no more light.

I always sang my song before I went to bed, but I had only heard my mother's once before. Her song was beautiful, but no matter how hard I tried to hold onto the lyrics, they kept slipping out of my grasp. I could only hold onto the song that I had been given; it was the only melody that made sense to me.

My brother stared at her with a look of melancholy. I knew it was because he understood that dad wasn't coming back now. I had asked Hyperion to sing me his song a million times, except he never would. He made silly excuses that he didn't like his singing voice and that he was waiting for his soulmate to sing it with him.

That night I spent sitting on the edge of my bed, looking up at the stars. One star in particular shone brighter than all of the rest. The North Star. My mom always said that it brought people home. It didn't matter where you were, you could always see it.

I took in its beauty while quietly singing my song. It seemed impossible that someone else out there was singing the same melody, waiting for me. I wondered where he was and what his life was like. Had I already met him? Could he see the colors too? My parents had believed I was crazy when I was younger because of it, but I knew what I saw. I watched my parents' clouds darken as they drifted apart. I have watched my brother's cloud bring light to everything around him. I wondered what color my soulmate's cloud would be, a light yellow? Dark blue? Something in between? I didn't know, but I bet he would be perfect. A guardian sent to watch over me and love me. A boy who could see the beauty in anyone and love them for their flaws. I knew that the person singing my song would lead a life more perfect than any angel could ever dream of.

Chapter Two

Ten Years Later

I grabbed my bag and crammed the remainder of my homework back into it. I cheerfully walked down into the kitchen to see my mother cooking breakfast and my brother seated at the table. Frowning a little, I noticed the deep orange hue above his head. His cloud had been getting darker and darker by the day, and I didn't understand why.

"Good morning, Tethys." My mother smiled, handing me a plate full of food. I gratefully took it and sat next to my brother.

"How do you think you did on that marine biology test you were talking about?" I asked, taking a bite out of my toast.

He merely shrugged and continued putting the finishing details on his essay. "How do you think you did on that math test?"

"Oh, I just know I failed that," I sighed. "I didn't know anything in that whole chapter, and I swear I studied!"

He scoffed and took another bite of his cereal. "If watching TV is your version of studying, then oh yeah. That's practically the only thing you did over break."

"Hey, I studied!" I hit his arm. "I even made flashcards."

"I'm sure you did," he rolled his eyes and ruffled my hair. "Well, you better hurry up and eat, because we have to go." He twirled his car keys on his finger to prove his point.

"I'm almost done!" I smacked his arm again and shoveled the last bit of toast into my mouth. "Give me a second."

"Well I am not going to be late, so hurry up." He smiled, grabbing his backpack. "I am going to have to drop you off at light speed if I don't want to be late for class."

"Whatever." I pushed past him slinging my bag over my shoulder and walked out the front door.

Chapter Three

After my brother drove off, I set off to my first class of the day: Chemistry. Mr. Aztec's lecture was boring as per usual, and I could not wait for lunch. As I sat there watching Aztec doze off on his desk, my thoughts wandered to the ever-growing mystery of soulmates. There were so many theories regarding the topic, but no one knew which ones were true. Many people believed that you can't ever leave your soulmate no matter what, but I knew the truth behind that one, after all my own father had left my mother. The others that understand that it *is* possible, don't leave for fear of being widowed or unable to financially support themselves.

The concept of people who have songs but feel no want for one is another big topic in our society. Some people say that it's selfish to do that to your soulmate, others say that they should have the choice. I didn't know how I felt about it; I've never understood how anyone wouldn't want a soulmate. Why would anyone ever *choose* to be lonely? And through all of that, there was the most terrifying thought of it all. Some people spoke of dying before ever even meeting their soulmate, or just simply never finding them. Some people said that you would know if your partner died, and that it felt like a piece of your soul was missing. I didn't understand how any of that worked, but every day I couldn't help but worry that something like that would happen to me or my brother.

I'd heard horrible stories where the person's soulmate was a terrible person, but they couldn't leave because they had become completely dependent on them for money. I couldn't imagine meeting the person you have been searching for your whole life, to find out that they only want to use you. That almost seemed worse than them simply leaving.

There were other rumors of people having more than one soulmate, but those were shut down almost instantly by the government. You had a song, and only one other person knew it. That was just how things were, and there was no changing that. Yet I had heard of people feeling love towards more than one person. Both claiming to know their song, and both following through. That was a rumor I was with the government on; it just seemed silly that *two* people could know your song. The Chanteuses would never allow something like that to happen.

Another one that always seemed to come up was meeting your soulmate only to find that they were not single, maybe even married. I wasn't sure how to feel about that one either. Wasn't everyone searching for someone who shared their song? How could they already be taken if the person didn't share their same tune? The Officials had insisted that none of these rumors were true, but I wasn't so sure for all of them. I at least knew they weren't right on the leaving one.

There had been many protests and riots on the freedom of choice. I supposed it would be nice, but I also figured that if you only had one special person, why bother? If only one person can complete you, why on earth would you want to get hurt at the hands of someone else? As I looked around the classroom, I wondered how many people here were each other's soulmates, and how many were what we liked to call 'Insiders.'

Tales had been passed around of these traitors living among us in secret. They weren't proven to be dangerous, but the thought still scared me. Insiders are regarded as outcasts; they're rare, but it has happened. I was thankful that no one in my family had been cursed that way.

The government had been hunting down the people without songs for years and after they were caught, no one knew where they went, or what happened to them. An Insider never came back after being caught. Some people said that they were sent off to war without choice. Others think that they were killed in the worst ways possible. I had my own theories on the topic, none of them good. Some people said that they were made slaves of Lieu and treated worse than the Outsiders. The most peaceful theory there was said that they were simply made homeless and thrown onto the streets to beg for food. Even though it wasn't exactly peaceful at all, it was a walk in the park compared to the others. I didn't blame Insiders for living in secret; wherever they were going, it was not pleasant.

I remember one day in elementary school, I had been playing ball at recess with my friend Drew when big trucks pulled up, all blasting sirens. I was confused at how terrified he had looked, but now it all made sense.

Men in uniforms came and grabbed him with rough hands. He had tried to run, but there were too many. They had dragged him away. I would never forget how his mother had come out sobbing and screaming.

Now I realized why it had happened, he was an Insider, but it still seemed horrible. He had only been eleven, I couldn't imagine how scared he must've been. He didn't even get to say goodbye to his family.

Once he had been extracted from the scene, everyone had been acting like I was infected. They were all asking if I had touched him or if he had spoken to me. I know that Insiders are not diseased now, but at the time I had begun to believe that he was sick and that was why they had taken him away so quickly. For years I expected to see him again. I even visited the hospital asking if he was in any of the rooms, but they said no one with his name had ever checked in.

My mother had been acting the same, asking if he had said anything to me or if I had touched the ball with too much exposed skin. I guess they believed that Insiders were contagious and might infect them with their low status.

Insiders didn't have a place in the ranks of Lieu. They were dangerous and outcasts never to be messed with. My society is all about status. If you were a standard citizen, you would lead a perfectly fine and normal life. If you were an Opulent, you would live a life worthy of a king, never consulting with any Standards except for a few rare exceptions, and if you were an Outsider you would live a life with poor conditions and little to no food. People believed that the Outsiders didn't have songs like the Insiders because they are too dangerous to be around. Most Outsiders died before they reached adulthood, some managed to scrape by long enough that they lived a little bit longer. Others stole and killed to live. Some say that if you're married to someone and they become an Outsider, you were stripped of your status as well. There are many ways to become an Outsider. Stealing was a big one, simply being born into an Outsider family, or breaking any of Lieu's rules were all strong possibilities. But once you killed or committed harm to someone in your rank or a rank above you, you were regarded as a Fugitive.

All Fugitives were caught and killed, after given years and years of jail time. Once their time was over, they are branded as a traitor and thrown off into the war to die. If you associate yourself with someone branded as a Fugitive, you were both as good as dead. Most Fugitives were too weak to even defend themselves after the brand, so they either die as quickly as possible or finish the job themselves. The thought sent chills down my spine and turned my stomach over.

I hadn't realized how long I had been spaced out, and that the bell had been ringing for quite a while.

I walked to lunch and quickly picked out my friends waiting at the table for me. I checked to make sure that all of their clouds were bright yellow, which eased my nerves.

"What took you so long?" my friend, Raven asked. She was always worrying about me, but I never worried about her, seeing how her cloud never went darker than orange. "Did Aztec hold you after class?"

"No, I just dozed off a little," I lied.

"Ah Tethys, you need to pay attention in class." Moon smiled at me and took a bite of her sandwich. She was blind in one eye and more positive about everything than I could ever be.

"Why bother? All Aztec does is sleep anyway," Violet grumbled. She was the sassiest and most grumpy out of all of us. But she was most definitely not sad in any way either. I always made sure to surround myself with people that had no chance of leaving me. There had been far too many accidents. That boy from elementary school had had a purple cloud, which at the time I thought nothing of. But now it made sense. He was always scared and jumpy, and I guess I always had associated purple as the color of fear. I wished I hadn't befriended him, but there was nothing I could do now.

"Wow, you're really out of it today. Are you okay?" Raven's gentle voice snapped me out of my thoughts once more.

"What? Oh yeah, I'm just really tired." I felt horrible lying to her, but I also didn't want to make her think I didn't trust her. I closed my lunchbox and leaned on my hand.

"Did you hear that the Sentinels are going door to door, demanding that people sing their songs?" Raven looked to make sure that no one was looking at us. "My dad thinks that they're looking for..." She paused again, lowering her voice. "Insiders."

That caught my attention, "You mean like...the ones without songs?" She nodded, looking a bit scared. I didn't need any further proof, if Lieu thought that going to such extreme lengths was necessary then they were obviously more dangerous than anyone had ever imagined.

"The thought of them living among us in secret terrifies me," Raven whispered, closing her lunchbox. "I hear that they're trying to overthrow Mr. Lieu, and end the rank system."

"I hear that all of the riots are being stirred up by them," Moon added. "My sister thinks that they're encouraging the Outsiders."

"The government has everything under control, and as soon as they rid us of those filthy rats, we'll have nothing to worry about." Violet smiled, looking surprisingly happy. I supposed she just liked to gossip. She was a higher-ranked Standard, meaning her father helped the Sentinels sometimes. "I bet that they're giving the Outsiders information on how to fit in."

"All of those ideas are ridiculous." I crossed my arms. "It's not their fault the Chanteuses messed up and forgot to give them songs." Sentinels, Officials, and Chanteuses were all considered Opulent citizens, performing duties for our nation. The Sentinels were our policemen, controlling the masses. Officials were government workers, assisting Mr. Lieu, and the Chanteuses were the singers. They had a special role in our society, working in the hospitals and singing to the children when they were born. They were the reason we had songs.

"Awfully defensive, aren't we?" Violet raised an eyebrow.

"I'd sing my song at full volume right here the second you asked me to, Violet. I'm not an Insider." I rolled my eyes. It's not like I had any sympathy for those wretches, but they didn't need to drag the Outsiders into this. I had nothing against *them*.

"Just…asking." She narrowed her eyes at me but remained silent. Then turning to Raven said, "The only good thing about being an Outsider is that *they* can marry whoever they want." She grumbled. "Plus, they can have more than *two* kids."

I sighed, "Then again, they don't get to have songs. Why bother having the freedom of choice, when you don't end up with someone you actually enjoy being with?" I pointed out.

"My mom says that they are only having kids so that they can outnumber us." Moon lowered her voice. "You know…so they can take us all out."

"Or they simply just want kids," I mumbled.

"Please, three kids is one thing, but seven sounds a little suspicious." Violet raised an eyebrow.

"Who told you that they were having seven?" I sighed; they were going pretty far with all of these assumptions.

"My dad helps the Sentinels in that area from time to time; he said that the families there were out of control." Violet crossed her arms, daring me to challenge her again.

"What about the Fugitives?" Moon asked; the atmosphere changed almost immediately. "I know that they're all either at war or dead…but what if there are some living among us too?"

"Please," Violet rolled her eyes. "You'd have to be smarter than the government to get past them, and does that seem like a very strong possibility to you?"

"I know but…do you think there are some still alive?" Moon was so quiet that I almost didn't hear her.

"The Officials would never allow that," Violet pointed out. "Fugitives don't even exist anymore; I bet they're just using them to scare us out of doing anything against the rules."

"What if that's where the Insiders are being taken?" Raven shuddered. "To go live with the Fugitives."

"All of them are dead, I'm telling you." Violet sounded bored. "Our society may have its faults, but they would *not* let something like that happen."

"Not everyone is as bad as you are at keeping secrets, Violet." I raised an eyebrow. "I wouldn't call it impossible."

Moon let out a scared squeak, then looked embarrassed as everyone turned to look at her. "Do you really think so…?"

I didn't want to scare her even more, so I lied. "You know what, you're probably right, Violet. What do I know?" Moon let out a sigh of relief, and we changed the topic.

After lunch, we all trudged back to our classes and sat through more boring lectures.

As I watched my teacher draw diagrams on the board, I gazed up at the cloud above his head. It was grey, a muddy color compared to the vibrant ones I usually saw. Even he was bored. The minutes seemed to pass by in hours of pain and agony. But eventually, after what seemed like days, the school day was over. I had to walk home today, which was fine. My brother had some 'thing' he had to do, or at least that's how he had put it.

When I walked inside, I found my mom sitting at the kitchen table, quietly humming her song. I decided not to say anything and just went upstairs. My brother wasn't home as expected, and I found myself sitting on my bed singing my own song. I still didn't understand why my brother's cloud was darkening all of the sudden; it didn't make sense. All of the rumors came into my head, but I quickly pushed them away again. My brother was none of those *things*, and I was sure it was probably nothing.

Hyperion poked his head into my room with a friendly smile on his face. I returned it, but it soon vanished when I looked up at the cloud above his head. It was a startlingly deep shade of indigo. He looked happy; I just didn't get it. Maybe my eyes were playing tricks on me? I wanted to believe that thought, but it seemed just about as logical as Raven being an Outsider.

"Are you okay?" I walked over, trying to keep my calm demeanor, and gave him a quick hug. I felt completely guilty and selfish about it, but I had begun distancing myself from him. I knew what was coming, and I didn't want it to hurt as much as my dad leaving.

"Of course, why do you ask?" He looked down at me, but there was no genuine confusion in his expression.

"No reason," I let my gaze fall to my feet, knowing that he was lying to me. I let him go, knowing that if he was anything like the others, he wouldn't be coming back. "H-Hyperion, can you sing me your song?"

He blinked in shock. "Sorry, but I have a lot of homework..."

"Please? Just once." I begged, terrible images coming into my head. Maybe it was just the light playing tricks on my eyes, but his cloud looked like a darker purple than before.

"I...Tess, I really have to finish my paper...maybe later, okay?" He gave me the most pathetic smile I had ever seen, but I let him leave.

I sat on my bed, staring blankly at my wall. I hoped that in the morning, I would find him sitting at the kitchen table, but if I didn't, at least I would be ready. My ability to see the colors had become a curse. One I wished would simply just go away. It had caused me to watch people leave, and my trust was wearing thin. I wished I could just be normal, that I couldn't see people slowly all dying away. It seemed that once they hit dark blue, that there was nothing I could do, and my brother's cloud had just gone from orange to a dark shade of indigo in only a day. There was no saving him, all I could do was watch him slowly fade away as well.

After a bit, I went down to dinner and found my brother sitting in the kitchen. I had never felt more relieved in my entire life.

My mother smiled at me as I sat down. "Hey, sweetie, how was school?"

"Good." I squeezed Hyperion's hand. He looked at me with a confused expression, but I didn't give him any form of an answer.

"Did you sleep okay last night?" She smiled at me, but I could tell there was something she meant by asking.

"Yeah...why?" I blinked, taking a bite out of my dinner.

"Well, it's just that the Sentinels were going up and down the street banging on doors. It woke me up, but I wasn't sure if you two had heard anything."

We both shook our heads, and I noticed that Hyperion looked very concerned.

"What did they want?" He stumbled over his words when he spoke.

"I think that they're searching for Insiders." She whispered. "Our neighbor said that they demanded her kids sing their songs immediately." She shuddered. "Those Sentinels scare the living daylights out of me. They're doing our house tonight, and I just wanted you to be ready."

Chapter Four

After dinner, we both returned to our rooms. I had just finished my homework when I heard a loud rapping against our front door. My mother called us downstairs and I quickly hurried down to meet her. Her tone had implied that this was important.

I found her standing in front of an open door, and three men dressed in bright yellow hazard suits outside of it. One of them took a look at me, then down at his list.

"Where is the third?" He snapped. The way he spoke made me feel nervous; what were they looking for? All of us had songs, so this was just silly. "I said, where is the third?"

"Sweetie, go get your brother." My mom said gently; she was trying to comfort me, I could tell.

I made my way back upstairs to his room. But when I opened the door, I stumbled backward. Lying on the floor was my brother's body, broken and bleeding. In his right hand was a note, and in his left, a shard of metal. I cupped my hand over my mouth to stop the scream as tears began streaming rapidly down my cheeks. There was a dark red streak of blood across his face, matching the color of the puddle he was laying in. The brilliant cloud he had once wore above his head was now reduced to a wisp of smoke. I was warned. I had seen it coming; I had known that this was going to happen, but it still hurt more than anything in my life, even my dad leaving.

I cautiously walked over and pulled the note gently from his hand. The paper was stained with crimson and had teardrops speckling it, crinkled from his fist. I opened it, barely able to see through my tears. It read:

Dear Cliffblazer family,

We are devastated to inform you of the death of James Nicholas Cliffblazer. James was one of many who lost his life fighting on the front lines. We honor his life, and our prayers are with your family. He died a soldier's death, one of honor and purpose. We thank him for his service to our wonderful nation, and ten years with the Lieu army.

To an amazing soldier and a great loss,

The L.A.O.

I bit my lip. It couldn't be. How could my dad *and* my brother, be gone for good? I had grown to hate my father for leaving me over the years, but I had never wished for this.

As I was leaving his room, I took one final glance back at him to see the last of the purple haze dissolving into the air.

I swallowed the lump forming in my throat and let out a small gasp as the sobs came. I couldn't stop them, he was gone. He was gone. How had any of this happened? I fell to my knees, clutching the note to my chest, the deep ache of it all finally sinking in. They were gone.

I hated the meaning death held. The permanence of its dark letters and the horrors it brought.

I felt as if the minutes were ticking by without me. My brother had killed himself…why? What had brought a happy Standard boy to do this to himself? To his family? What kind of life had he known?

I had every question in the universe, yet no answers. The curse that the clouds brought told me everything except for why. Why the world was this way, why it held all power and we held none. We were victim to its tragedies and its miracles. To its punishments and gifts. We were forced to accept it all with no complaint because that was how the world worked. It wasn't fair.

I let the sobs wrack my body; the pain of what had happened fully penetrating through. Tomorrow we'd have a funeral with no meaning because that's how it was in Lieu.

Meaningless words, meaningless promises. All left to break and never to build.

My gaze hardened on his still form and I somehow found the strength to stand. Taking one last solemn glance at my brother's body, I pushed through the door.

When I walked back downstairs, I found the three Sentinels looking highly unamused as my mom attempted to make conversation. As she spotted me, a relieved smile appeared on her face that quickly vanished as she noticed that I was alone.

I slowly shook my head, "Mom, he's…he's gone."

Her cloud darkened to blue in seconds, but I wasn't worried about losing her. The hue would always darken if people were feeling sadness. Her brown eyes watered already spilling the hot tears down her round cheeks. Watching the cold looks that the Sentinels were giving her for simply crying, filled me with a deadly rage, and I couldn't bear to see her cry anymore.

"Gone?" One of the Sentinels roughly pushed my mother aside. "What do you mean gone? Is he dead?"

I couldn't help it. Tears began rolling down my own cheeks, and I just barely managed to nod my head.

"We found one." The second didn't say anything else, just quickly marched upstairs. We all fell silent; I was so confused. Grief overwhelmed me as I stood there with the other two Sentinels.

When he walked back downstairs, he gave us both a nod, then turned to his fellow Sentinels.

"Sing." The third barked at me. That was the last thing I wanted to do right now, but I reluctantly obliged. It was against rule number seven to deny a Sentinel.

I quietly sang the words that seemed so far away from me now, my voice cracking from the tears, and my breathing was ragged. After I finished, they quickly left, murmuring with each other.

"What did they mean by 'we found one'?" My mom whispered to herself. I furiously wiped away the tears, not wanting to be near anyone anymore.

I ran upstairs, leaving her to her thoughts. None of this seemed fair, why did it have to be him? How could Hyperion have been one of those *monsters*? Begrudgingly, I thought of my song again, no longer wishing for someone to sing it with. All I had ever known was clouds going dark, and I was tired of all of these songs. These rules.

I cried in my room for hours, until I could only feel numb. I had seen this coming; I knew what was going to happen, it always did. I could've stopped him; I could've saved him.

Chapter Five

During first period, I sat there, blankly staring into space. I could only feel numb at this point; I had seen it coming. This wasn't surprising in the slightest…but it still hurt. I had done everything I could to ease the pain, but nothing worked. All I could do was watch as everyone else's clouds went dark too.

As I stared into space, I now knew that one of the rumors had been true. Insiders do die young, and at their own hands. My brother hadn't had a song, it was the only explanation that made sense to me now. Why he had refused to sing it at the annual check-ups every year, why he would never share it with me. The fury at everything in the entire world and nothing all at the same time was overwhelming. I needed to get my mind off of it, so for the first time ever, I decided to listen to Aztec's lecture.

"–and then that led to the attacks on the northern and southern United States in 1861 when we, unfortunately, lost countless men and women fighting to protect us. But as we know, one of the few soldiers who survived was a man named?"

"Henri la Beaulieu!" Everyone in the classroom chorused.

"Yes, a man that came from our French allies during the war, who would later build the wonderful society we know of today." I almost scoffed at that. Nothing about this was wonderful. "Henri picked himself up after watching so many of his colleagues die around him and did something so great that it would be remembered for centuries to come. But he would not know success until years after his death.

"In the year of 1897, when the Japanese fighter planes came and bombed one of our biggest ports, sending poisoned air and water down south towards what we know as the old Outsider towns. But Henri Beaulieu, despite his retirement, set up a simple and efficient system of young men who would either volunteer if they had a higher status, or be drafted if they were from the poor towns. Giving so many lives a newfound purpose. These men eventually fought us to freedom, and with Henri's new way of getting soldiers, we would have much more success in our later endeavors. After everything had been set right, Henri devised a way to ensure we would never have to face death, violence, or any sorrow ever again.

"He developed the system we know of today, with middle-class citizens such as yourselves, as Standards, and the high and in charge as Opulents. The Outsiders didn't come until about 1935, because of another incident regarding the Japanese and German soldiers this time. They came and bombed us again, leaving our country in ruins, and it took a while to recover, but we eventually fixed the ingenious system Henri had set for us. Even though it was way after Henri's time, the idea of ranks inspired people, so soon enough the system spread to almost every continent. But as you know some of the people in the British nations were not pleased with this. They thought we were taking away their freedom. The British rulers refused to join us causing the major war we fight today, known as?"

Many hands flew up into the air and some kid that I had never spoken to before, answered. "The Fissure War."

"Correct, and does anyone know who our allies are in this war currently?"

My hand shot up; this was easy. "France, of course."

"Very good. France is trying their best to keep the southern side of the British nation under control."

I sighed, wondering why this war had gone on for so long if we had such strong allies backing us up.

"Because our nation was built on half French, and half American, we learn French as our second language, and our singers are called Chanteuses. As we all know the Chanteuses serve a vital role in our structure. Being our singers, we don't know how they came about, but every year another person is reported and hired at the hospitals."

"How do they know what songs to sing?" Raven asked, raising her hand.

"They just do." He smirked, seeming proud. "I'd even call it magic."

He smiled at the class and continued, "We owe all of our thanks to Henri la Beaulieu, who founded our perfect nation and society known as Lieu.

"A long line of leaders descended from Henri, including our very own Head Official, Mr. Rafael Lieu. Because of these brave men and women, we have prospered for years since the war, and I don't doubt that the Fissure War will also be a success story."

I realized that I had been wrong in blaming them. And that Lieu was the only thing that was solid, something concrete and unchanging. Our society had a firm foundation, and that was all that mattered. I didn't care how many people's clouds went dark on me, because I knew that Lieu's never would.

At lunch, I didn't bother looking at my friends' clouds. I didn't speak, and no one asked. Raven was looking at me with concern in her blue eyes the entire time, but I refused to meet her gaze. It would only remind me of someone else's blue eyes. Eyes I didn't want to remember right now. I didn't need to deal with her worry anyway. I didn't think I could if I tried.

Everything was connecting in my head like puzzle pieces. He had been an Insider; he had been scared. But the mystery of his cloud darkening still didn't make sense. Maybe the stress of remaining a secret was just too much to keep?

I couldn't imagine living in fear every day. Waking up every morning, wondering if it was the day you'd be taken away. His death made me doubt the people around me. How many other people's clouds would darken by tomorrow? How many would be dead tomorrow? I didn't want the answer, but I made a pact that I would be careful of who I spoke to from now on. My parents had drifted apart in what seemed like seconds, and my brother had died suddenly without warning to anyone but me.

"Tethys?" Raven finally said something; I knew it would happen eventually. "You seem...quiet...are you okay?"

I gave a weak nod but didn't make eye contact. The thought of speaking to her brought tears to my eyes. *I was not going to cry here.*

"She's sad, because her brother died." Quite possibly the most annoying person in the entire school, Avalon, yelled over. "Honestly, got what he deserved. Filthy Insider."

"Yeah!" His useless sidekick, Charley, screamed.

I quickly stood up and walked towards the cafeteria exit as fast as I could, and as soon as I made it out of the door, I burst into a sprint all of the way to the bathroom. Everything seemed to make the fact that he was gone all the more real. These were people, real-life people, ones with emotions, fears, hearts, and I didn't know who I could trust anymore. I had no clue who would be announced as an Outsider tomorrow, who would leave tomorrow, who would be dead, and who would be hurt tomorrow. But I knew one thing, it wasn't going to be me.

Chapter Six

After the funeral service had ended that day, I went straight to my room. My mother didn't follow me, and I didn't want her too. It seemed that in less than twenty-four hours, my life had fallen apart. I dwelled on my thoughts, rethinking every situation that I could have changed, everything I could have done differently. He was gone…and I could have saved him.

After a while, my mother brought dinner up and wordlessly sat beside me on the bed.

"Hey…" She set her hand on top of my own, placing the plate on my nightstand. "Sweetie, I know it's hard, but…it'll all get better with time." Time. I was depending on it a lot these days…with time everything would be okay again. The world would fall back into place if I just waited, right? Wrong.

I looked down, not wanting to speak to her. My eyes went to her cloud, it was only a little darker, but I didn't even trust that anymore. "I know…" I mumbled, wiping away my tears. *I was so tired of crying.*

"He's happier now, I just...I just know it!" She heaved at her last words and took several deep breaths.

I didn't want to make this any worse, but I needed to know. "Remember when..." I paused, letting my gaze fall to the ground. "Remember when dad left? What did it feel like?"

She was silent for a long time, and just as I regretted asking, she spoke. "Like a part of me was gone...And now that he's...you know...I know that that part is gone forever." She choked on her tears, wiping her eyes. "I find it hard remembering my song most days...it's like it died with him."

"That must be awful..." I looked down, considering her words. "Do you think one day you won't be able to remember it at all?"

"I don't know." She wiped her tears stubbornly. "I suppose it's how we move on...it would only hurt to sing it again." I didn't agree with her; if I could hold on to my song I would. It would be my lifeline, my support beam. I didn't want to forget the one thing that we had once shared, then I would forget them altogether.

"I wish I could know when people are going, mom." I looked back down, unable to imagine forgetting my song completely. "That way no one could ever hurt me."

"I know, sweetie." She hugged me tightly, "but that wouldn't work, you can't know when a person is going to die."

I squeezed her back, but I wasn't listening to her words anymore. It would work, and I was never going to give myself another reason to hurt again. No more tears, no more pain. It would all fade away with him.

The next day at school, I ate alone. My friends were all looking for me, but I didn't want them to find me. I didn't want to know who would be gone today.

After I finished my lunch, I walked around outside waiting for the bell to ring. The front of the school was quiet and that was exactly what I needed. As I sat under a big tree, I looked down at my feet setting my bag beside me.

I wished that I could be normal, that in some reality, I wasn't cursed to watch people die. People were all the same, and the world would never have a single cloud that didn't turn blue eventually. Yellow clouds never lasted, and they never would. Even my soulmate seemed impossible now, like a dream too good to be true.

I was afraid that one morning I would wake up unable to remember my song, and unable to feel a part of my soul. I had been naive to imagine a perfect man when I was little, at least back then I hadn't known what it felt like to lose them and be helpless to stop it. What if my cloud was dark blue? What if my soulmate could see it, and decided I wasn't worth it? The scenarios flew through my head, each one making me more terrified than the last.

What if my soulmate was off at war, and I never got to meet him? What if he was a Fugitive? It was forbidden to marry someone in the lower ranks of our society, and you were always put with someone who was a Standard or higher. Only an Opulent could marry a down rank, which rarely happened. I had never seen the brand, but I had been raised to fear it with everything in me. If someone had it, they were dangerous and had killed at least a Standard. I let my thoughts wander for what seemed like hours until the bell rang.

Chapter Seven

The days flew by in what seemed like seconds; I had blocked out every one of my old friends, and only ever spoke to my mother. She was the only person I would ever get close to again. It seemed that as the years faded, so did the people around me. I had become numb to losing them, it was a feeling I had felt far too many times in my life.

Graduation came and went, and I was going into my first year in college. The thought of something new made me feel ecstatic. It felt like a fresh start from my old life, one where I could ignore the colors. I watched as my peers disappeared right in front of my eyes, but I couldn't be sad, not anymore.

I walked into my apartment and threw my bag by the stairs. Finals week was finally over!

I hadn't spoken to my mother in quite a while and decided to give her a call. I stared at the phone blankly as it rang, and rang...and rang.

"Hello?" My mother's voice came loudly through the speaker, making me jump.

"Hey, mom," I paused, checking to make sure that her tone was calm. "How are you doing?"

"Good, good. How are you liking your classes?" Her voice was cheerful, calming all of my nerves.

"They're okay," I laughed a little. "My professors are all a little crazy."

"That's astronomy for you." She chuckled. "We're all a little crazy."

"I didn't know that you majored in astronomy." I blinked, smiling.

"Not my major, but it was my minor. I sat right next to your...father." She paused awkwardly at her words. "Anyway, never mind me. Happy end of first year!"

"I know right, I can't believe it." I sighed. "I'm nineteen, isn't that crazy?"

"Oh, don't remind me." She let out an audible sigh. "What are you going to do for your twentieth?"

"That's not for a whole year, mom." I laughed. "Besides, I don't want to give you a heart attack by talking about it."

"Thank you," she chuckled. "Well, you better get some sleep. I will be doing the same."

"I get to sleep in!" I smiled. "Finally."

"Goodnight, Tethys. Enjoy sleeping in." I could almost see my mother rolling her eyes. "I love you."

"I love you too, mom." I pressed the hang-up button, all of my nerves melting away. Talking to her always seemed to calm me down. Even though finals were over, I was still feeling all of the stress of it. If I didn't do well, I might have to do a whole other year!

After changing into my pajamas, I read the book my mother had gotten me for my nineteenth birthday. The book wasn't very big, and I intended to get through at least a few chapters.

. . .

I hadn't realized how long I had been reading for, and it was nearly three in the morning. I sighed, putting it down reluctantly and getting into my bed.

As I switched off the light and got comfortable, I heard a crash from somewhere. My heart skipped a beat, but I convinced myself that it was probably just my neighbor's cat again.

As I finally began believing myself, I heard footsteps coming towards my room's door. Frozen in fear, I watched as my room door's handle began turning and I desperately reached for my phone. The door opened fully, and in walked a tall man dressed in all black. The room was dark, and I couldn't make out any of his features, except for his bright green eyes. He was looking right at me, and I knew he had seen me. I switched on the light, deciding that if I was going to die, I wanted to do it in the light.

I pushed myself backward as I took in his features. Everything about him was intimidating, a deep crimson scar tore through his right cheek starkly contrasting with the milky white of his skin. The youth in his face told me that he couldn't have been much older than me, maybe twenty, twenty-one. The startling green of his eyes was even more striking against the dim lighting of my room. His hair was blacker than smoke and curled every which way. In his left hand was a jet-black gun, but that wasn't what caused the sick feeling low in my stomach. Above his head, casting an aura of darkness across his face was a cloud in the deepest shade of black I had ever seen.

I looked back into his eyes, with tears filling mine. A feeble, "Please," was all I could muster as the fear consumed me. But my terror soon turned to confusion as I noticed his shaking hands. He looked more scared than I was, like he didn't want to do any of this.

He didn't say a word as he aimed the gun right at my heart. With trembling hands, he set his finger on the trigger. I squeezed my eyes shut, wishing I could tell my mother that I loved her just once more. So many people I had shut out, so many clouds that had turned blue. Was this all the world was meant for? To just die away eventually? I couldn't help the tears that began streaming down my cheeks; the tears that I had sworn to never show again. This was it. This was where my story ended, nothing but another cloud gone dark.

But instead of hearing a gunshot, a sweet melody escaped from his lips. A song so familiar, that I almost didn't process that he was singing it. His voice was the most beautiful thing I had ever heard in my life, and by instinct alone, I began singing along. His eyes widened, and he continued hesitantly singing with me. The way his voice harmonized with mine, sounded like we had been made to sing together. His voice was warm and low, a pure sound perfectly matching my own. When we sang the final lyrics, we both fell silent. He slowly lowered the gun, looking at me as if he was trying to memorize my features. As if he didn't fully believe that I was real.

"How…how do you know that song?" His voice was warm and smoother than butter. One that I didn't expect someone who was just trying to kill me to have. He had a strange accent—Australian if I had to guess—which made it all the more relaxing.

"What do you mean?" I whispered, terrified to speak with the gun still tightly clutched in his hand.

"How do you know that song?" His voice shook with desperation, and…anger?

"It's…It's my soul song." I explained cautiously, the anger in his tone had taken me by surprise and made me stumble backward. "It's…*our* soul song."

"Soul…song?" He looked genuinely confused; how did he not know if he had one?

"It's the song sung to you at birth." I backed up against my bed's headboard as far as I could. "One only you and your soulmate know…" He looked at me with wonder and confusion in his stunning eyes.

"Tell me more," he was inching closer to me, making me feel very uncomfortable. As he crept nearer, I noticed two silver earrings running through his right ear. "About…the songs." I didn't know what to say; he had a song so surely he had to know what it meant.

"It's the only song I can seem to remember…and I think you forget it once your soulmate is gone for good." I tried to push further against the headboard, but my back was already pressed firmly against it; I couldn't move. "W-who are you?"

His expression turned guarded, and his gaze fell to the sheets on my bed. "Unimportant...you?"

I blinked at his answer; he was the strangest person I had ever met. "I-I'm...Tethys."

He looked back up at me, his clear fascination returning. "Tethys." A smile crept across his face, filling his eyes with admiration. I was confused and a little unnerved by him being so close.

"Do I get to know your name now?" I felt trapped; I couldn't move back any further, and he was still clutching the jet-black gun tightly in his hand. The way he said my name with awe, his strange answers. He reminded me of a certain boy that I didn't want to think about right now. *Hyperion.*

His eyelids fluttered shut, letting out a deep sigh. I didn't speak, worried about angering him again. I also didn't miss the fact that he was fiddling with his gun's trigger. "Can you see them too?" His question was strange, leaving a lot of gray areas.

"See what?" I was starting to believe that he was crazy and wished I could call my mom or better yet, the Sentinels.

"The smoke." When he opened his eyes again, they were filled with wonder. "Yours is a bright, brilliant hue of yellow. It's shedding light on everything around it. Radiant and more beautiful than the sun."

"Wait you...you can see them too?" I blinked. Memories of people calling me crazy for seeing things that weren't real, all came back. I wasn't the only one after all. "The colors?" I was getting excited but kept myself composed, he was still holding a gun.

"What color is mine?" He asked eagerly, scooting farther onto the bed.

I looked into his hopeful eyes, wishing I could lie, especially after the way he had described my own. I didn't want to risk angering him, so I told the truth. "Black."

His face fell, and he looked down at the sheets once more. "I'm sorry."

"For what?" I blinked in confusion, instinctively trying to back up once more but soon remembering that I was as far as I could go.

He hadn't missed the fear in my eyes and how I had pushed away from him. "Ruining your soul song. It sounds like a wonderful thing that you deserve to have." He stood up and began walking towards my door.

His words took me by surprise, "W-wait, don't go." I didn't trust him, and I most definitely didn't love him, but I wasn't just going to let him leave. He was my soulmate whether I liked it or not, and I was not letting him just walk out on me like that. Besides, if he had a song, he had to be a Standard, meaning he hadn't killed anyone *yet*.

He turned back to face me, looking angry for no apparent reason at all. He watched as I cowered away from his stare with a bitter expression. "Please just let me go," he paused as if choosing his words carefully. "I don't find pleasure in watching people cower away in fear from me."

I blinked and with a shaky breath stood up as well. I had to hold back the '*then why did you just try to shoot me?*', but it wasn't easy. "I…" my gaze fell to the floor. "Please don't go." My thoughts went to my mother, she was the only person who hadn't left me. A small part of my heart whispered the *yet*, but I quickly pushed it away. The moment I met my soul mate had been built up my whole life and *this* was what had happened?

His eyes widened, "You…you don't want someone like me…I'll destroy your entire world. I…I'm a monster." He buried his face in his hands in frustration. "I shatter everything I touch."

I timidly walked towards him, my heart racing faster and faster. His cold aura seemed to cast shadows on everything around him, filling my room with a color darker than ink. I was shaking so badly that I could barely move, but I made myself take another step towards him. With trembling hands, I willed myself to take his hand in mine. He looked up with an emotion deeper than shock written on his face. Terrified was an understatement to how I was feeling, but I gave it a reassuring squeeze. His hands were freezing, colder than anything I had ever touched, but I held on tight.

"You're not shattering me." I smiled, hoping the terror wouldn't show in my eyes. "See?"

His hands were quivering in my grip, and his expression was unreadable. He didn't speak, but he also didn't let go. Up close I noticed a small scar down the middle of his bottom lip. I gently moved my hand and cupped his face with it. He was looking at me with fear, and I didn't miss the way he flinched when I raised my hand.

"What have you gone through? What happened to you to bring you to this?" I gestured to the gun in his other hand, making sure that the tone of my voice was balanced and none of the terror I felt showed. I needed to understand so I could help him, he clearly had been put through something dark enough to lead him to this.

He didn't answer, his startling eyes searching mine. He leaned into my touch, finally seeming to calm down a little. What could *they* have done to lead him to this?

"Can you...can you tell me more about these soul songs?" His eyes were filled with that same childish wonder that they had held before. It was the first thing he had said in a while, and I had forgotten how pleasant his voice was.

"To be honest, I don't know much about them." I genuinely wished that I could tell him more, he seemed so intrigued by them. "What's...what's your rank?" The question was insensitive, but I had to know. It was better for both people to just go on their separate ways then be dragged down to the level of an Outsider. Even though he had a gun, it didn't mean that he had killed someone yet. He could still be a Standard as long as he hadn't done anything, that or he was an Opulent who could kill someone as average as me in a heartbeat. I had only ever seen an Opulent on the broadcasts before, but judging by the way he was dressed, he wasn't one.

"Standard." The answer came so easily to him that I couldn't help feeling relief. I knew that the Chanteuses would never match a Standard with an Outsider, let alone one turned Fugitive, but I had to check. He hadn't gone as far as to kill anyone yet. The way he had acted about telling me his name had scared me into thinking that the Chanteuses had messed up somehow. I felt worlds more comfortable now, but I didn't miss the fact that he still had his gun out.

"So, what now?" I asked, excitement and relief coursing through me all at the same time. I had finally found my soulmate.

"Well, it's four in the morning," he looked over my shoulder at the clock. "I'll see you around, I guess." He turned to leave, seeming extremely eager to get out.

"Where?" I asked beside myself with happiness. I had just met my soulmate! Though I didn't want to disregard the shadowy cloud above his head completely. Years and years, I had spent carefully handpicking who I spoke to, making sure I never was hurt again, and here I was about to visit a man with the darkest cloud I had ever seen.

"Eastway Avenue, the cafe." He tucked his gun into his pocket. *Finally.* "Three in the afternoon."

I looked up at the black smoke above his head. "Promise you'll be there, okay?" I was risking way more than he knew with this.

"Okay…" he looked confused but didn't ask. When he left, I couldn't help but have flashbacks of my brother. I hoped that *he* would be there.

Chapter Eight

I woke up and almost didn't remember the events of the night before. It all seemed like a crazy dream, but the lingering chill in my hands was how I knew it was real.

I was feeling overwhelmed with relief and had so many questions. He hadn't killed anyone yet, but he had been driven to. I'd have to ask him about it, but a small part of me didn't want to know. I wanted to call and tell my mom everything, but something was stopping me. I didn't know how she would react.

I passed the time, by finishing off some of my homework. There was no way I could get it all done, but at least it was progress.

After what seemed like forever, it was finally three. A very small part in the back of my head was terrified; what if he was gone just like everyone else? I had begged him to stay, what was stopping him from leaving now?

As I made my way to the cafe, I started to notice the feel of my surroundings change. I was entering a downtown part of the city. I could tell.

The air became hazy from all the smoke, and as I passed the people around me, I took in the colors of their clouds. All of them were muddy grey colors; every single one was the same hue as the smog filling the air.

I nervously walked into the cafe, and to my relief found him sitting at one of the tables. I waved but he didn't look in my direction. He had his hood up, and his stare was fixed on the wood grain of the table in front of him. I walked over, sure that it was him by the pale color of his exposed hands.

"Hey," I tried to catch his gaze, but he didn't look up, only dipped his head a little. "This is an…interesting place to meet…" I sat down and caught a glimpse of his pitch-black curls popping out from underneath his hood.

"I usually come here to hang out," he muttered, keeping his gaze firmly planted in front of him.

I smiled a little to myself; I had forgotten how silky his accent was. I timidly reached out my hand, trying to get him to look at me. I cupped his cheek with it, but immediately pulled back when I felt a searing heat beneath my hand. I looked at him in horror, but he remained silent.

"What would you like? A coffee? Maybe tea?" The tone of his voice was casual, conversational even, making me worry even more.

"Um…I think I'll have tea." I tried to go along with his casual tone; maybe I had imagined it? I held out my hand again as if taking his own. He smiled stretching out his, but just as he tried to grab it, I pushed up his chin so that he was looking at me.

I was horrified at what I saw; his face was bloody and coated in dirt, it looked like he had been hit several times. His right eye was surrounded by a horrid purple hue. His expression was mixed, as I stumbled backward out of my chair. I fell to the floor, too shocked to speak.

He let out a light humorless laugh, clearly trying to cover up what had really happened. "You're so clumsy, Tethys." He walked over to me, still chuckling convincingly. He held out his hand, which I reluctantly took.

After I was back on my feet, he leaned in as if pushing the hair out of my face and whispered. "I didn't want you to worry. I'll explain outside."

I grabbed his arm, trying to look as calm as possible while made very aware of all the stares on us. I tucked my hand in the crook of his elbow and took care to maintain my normal expression. If there were any Standards in here, and they thought that he had hurt me, he could be sentenced for life. Hurting someone in your same rank was unacceptable and just as bad as murder in the society's eyes. As soon as the door shut behind us, I immediately turned to him.

"What happened?" I hissed, keeping my voice quiet, but the anger leaked through. This was way too much like my brother, and I was hating every second of it. "Standards don't fight, whoever did this to you could be put in jail."

He didn't answer for a long time, grimacing. "Walk." It wasn't a suggestion; it was a command. He started moving quickly down the street, but not fast enough that it looked suspicious. My grip on his arm was probably the only reason that I hadn't tripped yet.

"Where are we going?" I shivered a little from the cold of the streets. I clutched onto his arm tighter as we walked past a very bad looking group of people. I didn't know his name, I hardly knew anything about him, but I trusted him. Well, trust was a strong word. I was following him because if I wasn't with him, someone might try and rob me.

I saw a few people that were clearly Standards, but most of them looked like Outsiders, I shuddered at the thought and pulled myself closer to him. He didn't seem to notice my uneasiness, and if he did, he didn't say anything. We took a sudden turn that made me trip over myself a little, but thankfully I narrowly avoided falling once more. We were walking down a narrow alleyway, making me even more nervous. I started thinking of horrible scenarios in my head and was about to kick him and run when he opened a door hidden in one of the walls. This was crazy, he wouldn't tell me his name, and I was about to be locked in some wall room with him. He finally spoke.

"The people here are not the best lot," he mumbled looking up and down the alley. "I wasn't sure who could be listening…come, it's warm in there. Small but warm." He walked into the room without another word, and after hearing a loud scream, I quickly followed him. The room was smaller than I had expected, and at the corner was a fireplace, crackling as the logs withered away. There was a dusty scrap of fabric on the floor, maybe imitating a rug, but that was it. He moved to shut the door behind me as I heard another scream from somewhere. He seemed almost pleased with himself as he sat on the rug across from me.

"It's not the luxury an Opulent has, but it's warm." He gave a satisfied smile but grimaced in pain a second later at the movement.

"Do you…live here?" I looked around at the shabby room around me, it looked like it might collapse at any second.

"What? Of course not!" He looked like that was a ridiculous thought. "I'm a Standard, Tethys. And I do have standards." He winked a little at the pun, while I winced. Now was not the time for joking.

"So…how did you…you know?" I gestured to his face and all of the cuts and bruises.

"As much as I like this place, as I said earlier, the people here can get a little…violent." He sighed with the air any Standard would, melting away any remaining doubt I had. "I was unprepared."

"How'd you find this place?" I studied the makeshift fireplace and grime coating the walls.

"Knocked into the right wall, I guess." He shrugged casually. "Sorry for not notifying you earlier, I just didn't want my attacker to recognize me."

"Understandable." I inspected the bruises lining his pale skin. "I don't see why anyone would *choose* to hang out around here."

He shrugged again, a look of amusement spreading across his face. "I take it you don't like it here?" I nodded, distracted by how bad the cuts looked.

"We should get those cleaned up," I shuddered. "They might be infected."

He gave me a grim nod, looking like he was having a silent debate with himself. "Have you always been a Standard?"

"Of course I have," the very thought seemed silly. "Unless I got moved down from Opulent that doesn't seem like something that can happen."

"It's just…you seem like someone who would be an Opulent." He leaned against one of the walls, clearly in pain.

"Not sure what that is supposed to mean." I looked down, feeling defensive. I jumped a little as a third scream cut through the air. "Could we go somewhere else?"

He laughed a little, wincing. "They get really bad at night, and it's already starting to get dark. Though with all the smoke and haze, I don't think it ever really gets light here." He mused to himself. "We might be attacked if we leave now."

"Is that why you were walking so fast?" I blinked, moving closer to him and farther away from the door.

"You do not want to be caught out at night." A look of trauma played across his face. "That's when the Assassins come out."

I practically dove away from the door this time. "The...the what's?"

"Nasty gangs of people, only looking for trouble." He looked down, something on his face I didn't quite understand. "They hunt for weak Outsiders, or Standards who don't know what they're doing. You do not want to cross their paths."

I nodded, feeling beyond terrified. "Let's...let's s-stay inside, o-okay?" I stumbled over my words quickly tucking myself beside him. Silence passed between us, mostly out of fear for being heard. Only a few more screams for help echoed through the night, but that was enough for me.

"What's your name?" I felt after all that he had discovered about me, I at least deserved to know who he was.

He looked hesitant, which still confused me. "Asher." He muttered after a while. I smiled, feeling like I had finally gotten somewhere.

"Asher, huh?" I smiled. "Asher."

He gave me a weak smile, "I already know yours." Then with the same wonder in his eyes as before, he said it again. "Tethys."

"So...do you have any family?" I asked, leaning against the wall behind me. His presence beside me was comforting. He had figured out how to work these streets, and as a Standard, I respected that. I knew very few people who would even go near a place like this.

His expression was hard to read as per usual. He bit his lip, looking slightly pained. "Not anymore."

"I'm sorry..." I gently set my hand on his shoulder, making him flinch. People rarely died of anything but old age in Lieu, but it had happened. The Sentinels used to put out reports of missing people taken by Outsiders and later found dead. The thought made me think of my mother; I hoped she was okay.

Chapter Nine

When I woke up, the settings surrounding me were strange. I wasn't in my room; why was this place so empty? Why is there a man staring at me over there? As soon as I recognized Asher, I remembered everything. I was in a room the size of a broom closet, laying on a dusty scrap of fabric.

"How'd you sleep?" He asked rather cheerfully.

"Okay, considering our circumstances," I mumbled, looking around. "How'd you sleep?"

He just shrugged, "The screams kept me up." With how casually he said it I would've thought he was complaining about the dog keeping him up. "Now come on, we don't have much time."

"Time for what?" I blinked, standing up with him.

"To get you home, of course." He looked at me as if it was obvious. "You do want to go home, don't you?"

"Yeah, but…never mind," I mumbled, following after him. I slipped my hand into the crook of his elbow and let him lead me back out of the alley. I was eager to get out of there as soon as possible, but I knew that if we walked fast it would look suspicious. As he led me out of the broken-down city, a huge screen appeared on the building in front of us. A projection of one of the Officials, not Mr. Lieu himself.

"Attention all citizens of Lieu ranked big and small. We have a tragic announcement to make." He paused, looking genuinely sorry. "As you all know there have been Outcasts living among us, staining our society's records. We have begun calling these scoundrels Insiders. They are mistakes and extremely dangerous. If you or a loved one has had an encounter with one of these monsters, therapy will be provided. Please, for the safety of you and your neighbors, if you see any suspicious activity from someone you know, turn them in immediately. We will check if they have a song and go from there.

"These wretches have been stirring up the Outsiders, taking their perfectly content, happy lives, and turning them against us. For the betterment of our future, keep your eyes open, and be ready. They might come knocking on your door to take your daughters, your sons, your siblings, your loved ones. Stay safe and remember just how we got to this point. The danger these threats cause is a result of breaking the rules that have kept this wonderful nation stable and prospering for years. Let us recite the rules that so many soldiers, including our dear Henri, fought for to keep us safe.

1. *Never consult with an Outsider*
2. *Never break curfew*
3. *Never steal from someone above your rank or someone that shares it*
4. *Never harm someone from the same rank or higher*
5. *Insiders are extremely dangerous mistakes*
6. *Always keep your eyes open for the brand*
7. *Never, under any circumstances, deny a Sentinel or Official*
8. *The government always knows what's best for you*
9. *Never associate yourself with someone in the lower ranks*
10. *Sentinels have every right to ask and search to prove your innocence*
11. *All Insiders will be killed on sight*

"I understand that rule eleven is new, but I assure you that it would not have been added if not vital to the survival of this nation. Have a safe and secure rest of your day everyone."

The screen vanished as quickly as it had appeared, and I smiled. The Officials always knew how to make things better. I realized that Asher was clenching his fist, and gave it a reassuring pat.

"See? No need to worry anymore." He just gave me a weak nod and started walking again. I struggled to keep up with his brisk pace and eventually had to call for him to stop so I could catch my breath.

He remained silent and still until I began walking again. He slowed his pace but didn't speak a word. I knew him well enough at this point to *at least* understand that he would not go completely silent if it was not for a very good reason. I couldn't help looking around, worried that someone might be following us. He led me out of the small town, and into the part of the city that I had walked my whole life.

I finally plucked up the courage to speak, "Thank you…for not letting me…you know…die."

He let out a dark chuckle. "You're welcome. I trust that you know the way from here?"

"I do, but…aren't you coming with me?" Despite my best efforts, my eyes wandered to the black cloud above his head.

"I figured that after everything…" he shook his head. "Never mind, would you like me to come?"

My gaze fell to the floor and I felt my face reddening, "I…I wouldn't mind it." I found Asher's eyes studying mine as I looked back up at him. He almost looked…sad? I blinked in shock but decided against mentioning it. "Would you want to…it's silly really, but there's this field that I always used to go to, I mean of course you don't have to if you don't want to–"

"I'd love to." He gave me a warm smile, calming my nerves. "Where is this field of yours?"

"Oh, it's not far!" I felt giddy with excitement and began leading him through the city. He seemed a little on edge, which I found strange considering where we just came from.

As we turned the corner, an Official stopped us. I almost couldn't believe my eyes; Officials never left the shelter of their Opulent neighborhoods, and few Standards ever had the pleasure of actually meeting them.

"Hello, ma'am." The Official held out his hand, giving me a smile that was almost too perfect.

"Hello, sir." I shook it, looking around and realizing that Asher was no longer beside me. I wondered how long he had been gone, considering the Official's calm expression.

"You shouldn't be wandering the city alone, ma'am. With all of the riots and the *Insiders* on the loose, you never know who could be *one of them*." He said it all with a quiet and suspicious tone. "I know this will seem quite silly, ma'am, but I am afraid I am going to have to ask you to state your name, rank, and sing your song."

I nodded; this was just an Official, trying to keep safe. "Tethys Victoria Cliffblazer, Standard, sir." I took a deep breath and began singing the chorus of my song. I almost giggled as I realized it, *our* song. I sang my song just about a million times in my life, for teachers, Sentinels, my parents, it was nothing new, except now it felt different. As I sang the words that were impossible to forget, all I could think of was Asher's face, and how he had sounded singing it with me. It was almost a magical feeling; I was sure I was glowing. Wait. Asher! Where on earth had he gone?

"Thank you, ma'am. You may go on your way, but please." His expression went from a humorless smile to a very serious look. "Stay within the borders and follow the rules. These days they are the only things that will keep you safe."

"What borders?" I blinked in confusion.

"The ones dividing the ranks, of course." He said this as if it were the most obvious thing in the world. "I understand that before you had some freedom to go into the Outsider neighborhoods but trust me. We would not have done this if it were not completely necessary. No Standard is to leave their sections, the same goes for the Outsiders." He gave me a very fake smile but remembering that this was all for the best, comforted me. "It is to keep you safe," he laughed, but it held no real humor. "We can't have those miscreants running rampant, now can we?"

"I guess not." I looked down, feeling slightly reassured. Those parts of town were terrifying, dangerous, and run down anyway.

"You have a good rest of your day, ma'am." He dipped his head and continued on his way.

As I made my way to my apartment, I met several other Officials, all asking the same things. It was like they were loitering around, trying to catch any Outsider who wasn't supposed to be there.

I reached to unlock my door but found it already opened. Completely terrified, I opened the door, raising my hand as if I could defend myself. Seeing no one, I continued forward. The door to my bedroom was cracked open, and the light was spilling out from underneath. Ready for almost anything, I kicked open the door. Inside, I found Asher standing in the middle of my room. I let out a breath of relief and sat down on the bed.

"Where did you go?" I asked, kind of offended. "You just left me!"

"I continued to your apartment; I figured the Official had something personal that you wouldn't want me to hear." He shrugged, looking down.

"The Official hadn't even seen us yet!" I sighed, trying to understand. "Why are there so many of them just waiting around?"

"Searching for Insiders." He mumbled, something that might have been sorrow in his tone.

"You don't honestly feel bad for them, do you?" I questioned, trying to catch his eye.

"I mean, it's not their fault that the Chanteuses messed up." He gave me a small shrug. "I don't see why it's so bad, anyway."

"Asher, they are *mistakes*. Malfunctions in our society's perfectly structured walls." I sighed. "They're unstable and dangerous."

"You don't know that." He mumbled, letting out a deep sigh.

"I don't know for sure, but Mr. Lieu told us that they are, so they must be." I crossed my arms defensively.

He scoffed but didn't say anything else on the topic. "Did you hear about the border rules they are putting in place now?"

"Yeah, the Official mentioned it...I mean it's for the best, isn't it? Mr. Lieu wouldn't have put them in place if it weren't absolutely vit–"

"Vital to the survival of this nation, yeah, I know." He looked like he was struggling to hold back the eye roll. "Doesn't all of this seem...I don't know, a bit excessive?"

I blinked taken aback, "Never doubt the Officials, trust me. In a week or less, all of this nonsense about rebellion will be gone."

He raised an eyebrow but dismissed the topic almost as quickly as it had begun. "Have you visited your mother yet?"

"No, why?" My gaze fell on my phone; I hadn't given her a second thought ever since the broadcast.

"Well, I guess I just assumed that you would be worried about her." He followed my gaze to my phone.

"How about we go to this field of yours tomorrow, and you can check in on your mom, okay?"

"Okay, thank you…Asher." I smiled up at him, and he gave me a weak grin before leaving.

Chapter Ten

After I finished speaking to my mother, I got into my pajamas. It had been such a tiring and stressful day that I figured I would have no trouble falling asleep. With that small comfort in my mind, I drifted into a restless sleep. My dreams were filled with terrifying scenarios involving the Insiders and revolting Outsiders. What if those scary gang leaders somehow got into the city? He had called them Assassins.

I tossed and turned in my sleep, nightmares filling every second of my dreams. I dreamt of my brother and what had happened to him. *What he had done.* Broken, bleeding silhouettes played across my visions. Screams. My mother's body lying on the floor, crimson spilling from her.

"Mom!" I screeched, but I couldn't run. I looked down and saw people with navy clouds trying to drag me down, deeper into the dark waters. My strangled screams were lost in the sounds of gunshots. I watched as she was tortured, crying out for me, but I couldn't reach her. I let out a shriek as the clouds began to cover her, her screams getting fainter and fainter—

I woke up in a cold sweat; it was still dark outside. I checked my clock and sighed falling back onto my bed. It was one A.M. I reminded myself that none of it had been real, and drowsily walked over to the society's handbook. Yes. We have a handbook. It states the rules—or the original ten at least—and the phone number of every citizen in the area. I searched the book for the name Asher, but I realized I would get nowhere if I didn't have a last name. As I was about to flip the page, my gaze fell on a name that had been crossed out in red ink under the Outsider section. *Griffin Chainbreaker*. I didn't remember crossing it out, and I wondered if an Official had come to update it and I simply didn't remember. They would cross out your name in black ink if you died, but never in red. I blinked in confusion, and out of curiosity, flipped to the back page of the book. In blood-red letters was the word *Fugitive*. Fear surging through me, I read down the list of every Fugitive that had ever lived. All of them were written in the same crimson letters and crossed out with black ink to signify death. All of them except the name *Griffin Chainbreaker*.

I fell backward to the floor, my heart pounding in my chest. It must have been a mistake, no Fugitive lived after the brand. After every Fugitive death, they would broadcast it, and tell us to cross out their names. Maybe I had just missed the broadcast…yeah, that had to be it! I quickly closed the book and set it back on the shelf.

It must've been hours I was trying, but I could not fall asleep again. I was too scared; why had that *one* Fugitive's name not been crossed out? Lieu never let Fugitives escape alive; they would never allow something that dangerous to happen. For the tenth time I tried to convince myself of that, and to just go back to sleep, but to no avail. I sat up in my bed and turned on my light after hours of useless attempts at rest. My eyes fell on the book sitting on my shelf. Defeated, I walked back over to the table and picked up the book. I brought it back over to my bed, flipping mindlessly through its pages until I got to the last remaining few: Outsiders and Fugitives. Despite my best efforts, I found myself studying the Fugitive page. At least a hundred names were all crossed out in black ink, all except Griffin Chainbreaker. I flipped to the next page and paused. In handwriting that was not from the Sentinels, was a bunch of information on this Griffin. I cautiously read it, scared of what I might find.

He was born to an Outsider family because his father had married his mother then stole something. I sighed, shaking my head a little. I had always thought of it as selfish to do that to your spouse.

I read on, my curiosity getting the best of me. Both of his parents were dead, he had been the eldest of six. *Had.* Three brothers and two sisters it looked like. I blinked, thinking of Violet's words. *Six kids*, now that was a lot for such a low ranked Outsider family. I couldn't imagine how all five of them could be dead, and it didn't talk about him like he was too. He had become a Fugitive at as young as eight years old. I winced thinking of a boy that young, killing someone in cold blood. He had been sentenced to five years, then branded and shipped off to war. I blinked, he must have been caught before it got too serious, because, five years, though it was a lot for someone that young, wasn't as bad as it could have been. My gaze fell on a chart I had never noticed before at the bottom of the page, it was once again written in the scrawly and messy handwriting that couldn't have belonged to a Sentinel.

Griffin Chainbreaker
Date of Birth: 7/31/37
Current Age: 21

Age marked as Fugitive: 8
Amount of jail time: 5 years
Time served in the war: 3 years

I paused in terror when it used the words *current age*, which meant that he was still alive, yet they implied that he was no longer serving at war. Then words I had never seen before, confirmed my suspicions.

War Criminal: 16 years old

This Fugitive was still alive, and he had become the first one ever to survive the brand and escape the war.

Chapter Eleven

I felt like I knew a secret that wasn't meant to be known, one that could very well get me killed. I didn't understand why my book had that extra section written in it. Had Mr. Lieu found out about the clouds? Had the Fugitive found out about the clouds? I shuddered at the thought, and almost didn't leave my house that morning, but I had promised Asher I'd meet him at the field. I didn't feel safe and was sure that if I was confronted by the Sentinels I would crack under the pressure. Nonetheless, I made my way to the field despite my worries.

I realized as I climbed up the hill towards the big tree that I always sat under when I came, that Asher hadn't even asked where the field was. How on earth was he going to find it? After sitting there for fifteen minutes, I debated on going home just in case he was there, waiting for me. But then again, what if as I left he arrived? I sighed, feeling frustrated as I realized he hadn't even given me a time! He could have meant this evening, noon. Heck, he could have meant midnight! I picked myself up off of the grass, beginning to question just how compatible we were. I wasn't a clean or order freak, but I at least needed someone who could focus for one second! Anger swelling in me, I began to trudge back down the hill. He hadn't exactly stood me up, but it sure felt like it. How on earth had he expected to find the field and meet me without setting a time or even knowing where this place was? Feeling dumb, I began the path back to my apartment. I had homework to do anyway.

I stuck my key in the door, but right as I went to turn it, the door creaked open. I blinked in shock, this had happened once before and it had ended up being Asher, but with the knowledge I now had about Griffin, I couldn't help the fear that surged through my body. Someone had written the extra information in my book, someone had wanted me to know about this Fugitive that had survived, and someone had been in my apartment or was currently in my apartment.

I crept inside, my heart pounding in my chest. The door to my bedroom was wide open, and no one was there, so I continued to the kitchen grabbing a shoe. I wasn't sure how much protection it would provide, but all the same, it made me feel safer.

I entered the kitchen sure my heartbeat would give me away. The light was off, and the door was wide open, but considering the layout of it, there could still be someone hiding. Terror was coursing through me, and it was getting noticeably harder to breathe.

Cold arms wrapped around me from behind, making me scream, drop my shoe, and throw a punch as hard as I could behind me. I heard several grunts in pain, as my fist met its target. I turned around, ready to punch again, but paused when I recognized my attacker.

There standing in front of me with a bleeding nose was Asher. "What was that for?" He complained, clutching his nose.

"You startled me," I mumbled defensively. Then remembering my anger with him, crossed my arms.

"That was the goal," he winced, giving me a playful look. "Boy, you can punch."

I looked down, not wanting him to see my smile. "Is it broken?"

"I don't think so," he crossed his eyes, trying to look at his nose. "Probably not, but could you get me a paper towel or something?" He pinched his nose, trying to stop the bleeding.

I walked into the kitchen and grabbed a paper towel. I turned to give it to him, but right before I handed it to him,

I heard a gigantic bang from somewhere next door. What I did next, was purely on accident and I am not proud. I kneed him in the gut.

"Oi!" He crumbled, hands clutching his stomach. "Why are you doing this to me?" He pleaded, desperately.

"I'm sorry, it's just how I respond to being startled," I mumbled, feeling slightly sorry for him.

"Well then, stop being startled!" He grunted, his voice much higher than it had been before. He stood up wincing, and still guarding his stomach. I had to hold back a laugh as he awkwardly hunched over, one hand clutched over his stomach, and the other trying to shove the paper towel up his bleeding nose. "Why are you so on edge today?" His voice was shrill like a bird's.

"I–" Before I could answer a hard rapping sounded from my front door. I wasn't startled this time, only confused. Who was knocking on my door with such urgency and force? A small voice in the back of my head reminded me of the information in my book that wasn't supposed to be there.

I cautiously peeked through the peephole, and almost passed out. There, right outside of my door was a Sentinel covered in what looked like blood. Panicking, I sprinted back into the kitchen where Asher stood bleeding and yanked him over to the broom closet.

"Look, I will be made an Outsider if they see what I did." I couldn't breathe, my heart was racing in my chest. The look he gave me, took me by surprise, he almost looked…hopeful? "It was an accident, Asher! You have to hide." The banging came again, except louder. I was getting more and more anxious and the Sentinel's knocking shook the door. He bit his lip, looking torn. Frustration and terror overwhelmed me as the banging became more consistent, and despite how much worse things might get, I shoved him into the closet and slammed the door shut.

When I opened the door, the Sentinel's eyes were filled with fury. "What took so long for you to open the door, ma'am?" His usually composed manner was wild, he looked on the verge of insanity.

"I…what was that noise?" I paused, forming something that wasn't quite a lie. "I thought an Insider might be outside, so I was scared to open the door."

The Sentinel nodded slowly, "Smart plan, but let me assure you, you won't have to worry about an Insider around you for quite a while." He paused, obviously trying to hold back a smile. "It appears that your neighbor has been lying to you and your fellow citizens. Mr. Fellows was an Insider, and believe me, he will never be able to endanger you or your family ever again." *Mr. Fellows...where had I heard that name before?* Then it clicked. *Mr. Fellows had been the school's math teacher for years.* A pang of sadness hit me, I had been close to him, he had always been so nice. *No.* He was dangerous and unstable. He must have been faking it waiting to...um...hurt me! Yeah, kill me and my mom.

"Please state your name, rank, family members, and song." The Sentinel's voice pulled me from my thoughts.

I tried my best to steady my breathing. *He didn't know about the extra writing.* "Tethys Victoria Cliffblazer, sir. Standard. Mindy Cliffblazer is my only living relative...my mother, sir." I paused taking in a deep breath before singing my song, carefully keeping my breathing in check.

"Have you met your intended partner?" He snapped, taking no effort to keep his voice calm.

My smile faltered as I remembered Asher. I hoped he would stay quiet, accident or no accident, I had technically hurt someone in my rank, and I would have my rank stripped away and be thrown onto the streets as an Outsider to die. "Yes, sir."

"Your partner's name, rank, nationality if different, and location." He looked me up and down slowly, pausing. "Aren't you quite young?"

"I'm nineteen, sir." I was calming down, and he gave me a small nod to proceed. "His name is Asher, he's a Standard. I…I think he's from Australia, and I…I don't know where he lives, sir."

He tutted, looking down. "You need to find out last name, family members, his definite nationality, and where he lives, ma'am." He dipped his head. "Until next time."

I closed the door, letting out a breath I hadn't realized I had been holding in.

"Can I come out now?" Asher's muffled voice came down the hall.

"Oh, right!" I ran to the closet and quickly opened the door. "Sorry…"

"It's okay," he rolled his shoulders, stretching. "Not the first time I've been shoved into a broom closet."

"Really?" I blinked, in confusion.

"It's a long story." He waved his hand, walking out of the closet.

My gaze fell on his still bleeding nose, "You're not…you're not going to turn me in, right?" I was terrified of him leaving, of being an Outsider…of being abandoned and hurt.

He gave me a warm smile that melted all of my fears away. "Of course not, Tethys. It was an accident." He chuckled. "I'm not an Opulent." He paused, his smile dwindling. "Just so you know…if you were to… if I was…" He went silent, struggling to speak. "If you did somehow become an Outsider I…I wouldn't leave. I would stay," he smiled. I couldn't help the grin that spread across my face, but I tried to conceal the real joy of his words inside. He didn't know how much him staying meant to me, especially after my dad and my brother.

"I'm guessing you heard the Sentinel…" I looked down.

"My last name is Walker, I am from Sydney, Australia, and I live not far from the Outsider towns." He sighed, "The air is not very clean, but my home is nice." He gaze turned cold, melancholy filling his tone. "I…I had five siblings…none of them survived the smoke inhalation and polluted waters. My mom works as a Chanteuse and my father was just a Standard. He…he also didn't make it."

"So, it's just you and your mom?" I looked at him with understanding as he gave a small nod. "Hey, that's okay." I nudged him, trying to cheer him up. "One day we're going to have a family of our own. Where no one can be sad."

He gave me a sympathetic smile as if he wished such a world existed, one where sadness was nothing but a dead memory.

"Maybe."

Chapter Twelve

I decided it would be best if Asher and I just ignored everything that had happened that morning and left to get coffee at a nearby cafe.

"So," he whistled looking around the streets. "What are you majoring in?" He gave me a little nudge with a smile. My gaze flickered to the pitch-black cloud above his head as I answered.

"Astronomy." I looked back at him and could tell he had noticed. He quickly looked down, some unreadable expression on his face. The cloud above his head was constantly casting shadows around him, and a harsh reminder of how dangerous all of this could be. "What are you majoring in?"

He didn't reply, and I could tell he wasn't very eager to answer. "Where is this cafe you were talking about?"

I blinked, shaking off the sudden discomfort. "Oh, not far." I sighed, feeling like the more he knew about me, the less I knew about him. "So, before your family...you know...what were they like?"

He looked up at me surprised. "Well," he paused, biting his lip in thought. "My siblings were all wild and loud." He chuckled. "Very loud. I..." he paused as his smile dwindled. "I didn't get to spend much time with them. The truth is I spent most of my days with my father."

I smiled, feeling a pang of jealousy. I had barely gotten to know my father before he up and left. "Were you two close?"

He furrowed his brows, looking straight ahead. "No."

I blinked, taken aback by his answer. I decided not to press any further. "What was your house like?"

"Small," he paused as if trying to find the best words to describe it. "Extraordinarily loud," he smiled, letting out a small chuckle. "We didn't need much to be happy. As cheesy as it sounds, we only needed one another to get by."

I smiled, thinking of the days before my father left. "I get that." Through the years, so many people I had considered lifelines had become strangers to me. I wanted to know Asher; I didn't want *him* to be a stranger, too. "What was he like? Your father."

His expression went cold, a look he seemed to get every time I mentioned his father. "Ambitious, persistent...he never seemed to know when it was too much. Nothing was ever good enough for him." He looked down a clear hatred in his tone.

I gave him a weak smile, trying to find a way to change the topic. "What did you do for fun most days?"

He looked back up at me, raising an eyebrow. "For fun?" I nodded, thankful that he had seemed to calm down a bit. "Train."

"For...for what?" I stumbled over my words, surprised by his answer.

"It's best if you don't know." He said, with a tone of finality.

I sighed. *Back at square one.* "Asher, you're going to have to tell me something eventually."

He didn't answer, just continued walking in silence. My thoughts went to the broadcast, and I tried again at a conversation. "That broadcast was reassuring, wouldn't want deadly Insiders out on the loose."

"What makes you say they are deadly? Have you ever come across an Insider that tried to harm you?" He looked genuinely curious, and completely unaware of how much that memory hurt me. I had met an Insider and he had been nothing but nice to me, which made it so very hard to hate him. But I *had* to hate him.

"No," I mumbled, looking down. "But I know that Mr. Lieu would not have created rule eleven if it had not been necessary."

He scoffed, "So the killing of innocent Standards who simply don't have songs is necessary to you then?" He gave me a humorless smile, "I must admit, they train their puppets very well."

"I am not a puppet," I huffed defensively, before getting my tone back in check. "They have always given everyone a choice."

"A choice? That's what you call this?" He snapped, his tone unsteady. "This pretty little cage that they have trapped you in, is a choice?" The sudden anger caught me off guard. What had I done to provoke him? "Why do you think so many Outsiders die young? Why do you think people are driven to kill?" He took several deep breaths, but it was too late, I could almost see the chains breaking. He was about to burst, and I did not want to be there to see it. "Desperation does horrible things to a person, Tethys. Unspeakable things."

I didn't like the look in his eyes, but I forced myself to speak up. "Fugitives have no excuse for what they do!" I shot back, pushing forward a little.

"Oh really?" The look in his eyes was positively deadly. "Is that why the Assassins are all saints in your mind? Because they're only killing people that don't matter? Disposable lives, right?"

"Of course they're not," I mumbled, looking down. "I never said any of that."

"Tethys, you know nothing about suffering. You know nothing of what goes on out there! What is happening with the Fissure war!"

"You don't either!" I finally screamed. "You have no right to tell me what I have and haven't experienced, especially when you are just as clueless as I am!"

He threw his arms up in frustration. "Doesn't this bother you?" He gestured around us. "Doesn't any of *this* bother you? Don't you want to choose? Don't you want to be able to decide where your life is going, instead of being confined by some ridiculous rank? By some family name?" He was backing me up against a wall. "Am I the only one who thinks there is something more? Beyond Lieu, beyond these…these rules!"

"The rules are here to keep us safe." I blurted out by force of habit.

"Safe?" His voice was unsteady, almost to the point of yelling. "That's what you think *this* is? Tethys, being confined and told what to think, is not keeping you safe. It's keeping the Sentinels safe! Haven't you ever been hungry? Not just that, but starving?" He paused, a deadly fire in his eyes. "Have you? The Officials aren't keeping us safe, *they* have never cared about what happens to us! Why do you think gangs like the Assassins roam freely, with no repercussions?"

"I–" My words failed me. I didn't know what to do. I was being cornered. Forced to question the only constant in my life.

"They couldn't care less about us," his voice didn't soften; the look in his eyes held no remorse. "You spend every second looking at my cloud, Tethys! At the colors above our heads, when you should be focusing on how brainwashed they have made you!" I looked down, feeling guilty. "Keeping you in these walls, forcing you to follow these rules. You're like a caged animal. All you care about is what they have told you to think, and these ridiculous clouds!" His voice was unsteady, but his stance was anything but that. He was towering over me with his shoulders squared. I was now pinned flat against the alley wall. "All you seem to see is the colors! Is that all that matters in your twisted reality? There are people behind these clouds, Tethys! Do you even notice anymore?"

I cowered as he finally yelled and shielded my face. For someone that I hadn't known that long, he had just read me like an open book, and I hated him for it. He was forcing me to think about the people whose clouds had gone dark. He was forcing me to question the society for the first time in my life.

I looked back at him through my fingers, my heart racing in terror. The anger in his eyes melted away, and he let out a deep sigh, shaking his head. He turned away from me, muttering to himself. It was so quiet I couldn't make out what he was saying. He sounded frustrated, but with whom I didn't know.

I cautiously crept away from the wall, feeling slightly better. I looked around to make sure that no Sentinels had seen that whole explosion. As I got closer to him, I could make out a few of his words. "I'm sorry…I'm sorry…I'll be better…I'll do better." I blinked, unsure of who he was talking to. When he turned back to face me, I flinched. His eyes held a deep sorrow. "I can't do this anymore."

"Can't do what?" I paused, making sure to keep my breathing in check.

"This." He gestured between him and myself with a frustrated sigh. "I can't go any further with this until you understand."

I let out a nervous laugh, "So you have a short temper, everyone has one, Asher. I hardly think that—"

"Not my temper." He cut me off, letting out a deep sigh. "You need to understand…everything."

"O-okay…" I gulped, not sure if I should be worried or relieved. He was finally going to tell me everything about himself. Something I should have known long ago.

"Follow me." With that, he walked off, down the streets towards roads I had never seen. Maybe I just hadn't noticed them before. He took me down winding gravel roads, and through alleys going deeper and deeper into what looked like an abandoned Outsider city. I choked on the air as soon as we reached it. This was an abandoned town alright, one that had been evacuated for a reason.

Asher seemed unaffected by the horrible air conditions, while I was taking ragged and strangled gasps of it.

"Hold your breath, we're almost there." He said gently, trying to reassure me. I couldn't imagine why he chose to live here. I guess it was far away from the society he seemed to hate so much.

He led me up to a very shaggy looking building, it was small, with holes and tears at every turn.

I blinked, taking in the horrible sight. No one, not even Outsiders were forced to live in these conditions. "You're a Standard, you shouldn't be living here."

"I choose to." He said simply. "Come inside, we have some form of fresh air in there."

"We?" Before he could answer, the door burst open and out ran a plump woman slightly taller than me, with dark skin, curly black hair, and deep blue eyes. She had wrinkles and gray streaks filling her dark hair from age, but her eyes held a youthful twinkle.

"Oh, thank goodness you're home, Gr—"

"Mum! I'm okay, we should get her inside though." He seemed flustered for some reason and giving her son a confused look, she dragged me inside. Her hands were calloused to the touch, but she handled me with such care I knew I didn't need to be afraid. I looked up at Asher's cloud, and couldn't help but smile, his cloud was at least a few shades lighter just at the sight of his mother.

"Whom might you be, dear?" She instantly went to inspect me for any bruises, I guess.

"My name's Tethys." I blinked, looking up at her kind face. She looked nothing like Asher, except for her unruly hair, though his was much darker. If they hadn't said it, I never would have guessed that they were related. "Who are you?"

"Mary." She smiled giving her son a tight embrace.

"Wow," I mumbled taking in their extraordinarily different looks.

"Well, you are just the most precious thing, aren't you?" She walked over to what I guess was their kitchen humming. "So how do you know my baby boy?"

Asher groaned a little with noticeably redder cheeks. I chuckled to myself, unsure of how I had ever felt scared of him. "Well, he's actually kind of, I guess you could call him my…my soulmate." It was my turn to blush.

"Oh, I knew it from the moment you walked up! I can't believe my Gr-"

"Mum!" His voice was much higher, and he pointedly cleared his throat.

"Can't I be happy?" She put her hands on her hips, glaring at him.

"We're here to discuss the current…situation." He mumbled, looking down.

"Current?" She scoffed. "You mean permanent."

"Wait…what's wrong with Asher?" I blinked, looking between the two of them.

"Who?" She looked just as confused as I did now.

Asher walked over to his mother and whispered something in her ear. He gave me a weak smile before taking a seat on the floor.

"Oh! That makes much more sense." She gave me a smile that warmed every inch of my body and grabbed an apple from their fridge. "Hungry, sweetie?"

"No, thank you though." I looked at Asher for answers, but he didn't meet my gaze.

"Now," she gave me a serious look. "Let's set everything straight."

Chapter Thirteen

"I used to be a Chanteuse," Mary explained calmly. "Then I married his father, and well." She sighed. "Having no need to sing anymore, I retired. His father was a great man, he...he provided for us as best he could." She and Asher shared a look that I didn't get. "I sang to you," she smiled. "I remember it like it was yesterday. You were so small...so innocent, there was a certain look in your eyes, I just knew." I looked over at Asher and took his hand in mine, squeezing it.

"So, you used to be an Opulent?" I blinked, unable to imagine her being on the same level as the Sentinels.

"Yes, I was an Opulent." She looked off, seeming to remember something.

"Why would you give that up?" I asked, knowing what she was going to say.

"No matter who your soulmate is, no matter how far away they may seem." She smiled, warmly, looking from me to Asher. "You will always find your way back to them."

. . .

I spent several days with Asher and his mother, there was just something about them that made me feel safe. But a deep dread filled me, thinking of my mom and what might be awaiting me when I got home.

"So, did you grow up here?" I looked around at the abandoned town.

"Yes." Asher smiled, continuing forward. "See that little building over there?" He pointed in the direction of a torn down brick building.

"Yeah," I blinked, trying to find one remarkable thing about it.

His eyes filled with wonder, "It used to be a massive skyscraper, one you could see from almost anywhere in the town- Oh! Do you see that oval-shaped structure?"

"That one?" I smiled at his enthusiasm; I hadn't ever seen him this peaceful.

"Mmhm, we used to have massive parties where we would roast hot dogs and s'mores for hours on end!" He seemed to be reliving some of the best memories of his life, and I watched as not only his smile got brighter but so did his cloud. It was still dark grey, but it was progress.

"It sounds like you really love this place," I gave him a warm smile. "How did it get so wasted?"

He looked down, his smile fading. "The..." he choked on his words. "The Japanese and German soldiers, they...they took everything." His eyes went dark, I could tell he was remembering horrible things. I didn't know how to respond, but I didn't want him to relive it. I could tell it was hard for him, and I couldn't imagine my whole neighborhood being destroyed, and never being fixed. We kept walking, except in silence this time.

I was about to attempt at conversation again when a huge projection appeared on a broken building in front of us. This one was hosted by Mr. Lieu himself, so it had to be important.

"Attention citizens of Lieu, we are now facing something that could very well tear apart the seams of our lovely nation. As you may know, some citizens who have everything they could ever want and more, are unhappy. They are known as Insiders, people who had perfectly happy lives, and threw them away. For what? A rebellion? Murder? Whatever they want, it will only harm the good people left in this world. These monsters are being tracked down before they can track you down. They will kill everyone you love in cold blood. These creatures will stop at nothing, they now pose more of a threat than the Fugitives. Their goal is to encourage the breaking of our sacred rules. Rules people gave their lives to enforce!

1. *Never consult with an Outsider*
2. *Never break curfew*
3. *Never steal from someone above your rank or someone that shares it*
4. *Never harm someone from the same rank or higher*
5. *Insiders are extremely dangerous mistakes*
6. *Always keep your eyes open for the brand*
7. *Never, under any circumstances, deny a Sentinel or Official*
8. *The government always knows what's best for you*
9. *Never associate yourself with someone in the lower ranks*
10. *Sentinels have every right to ask and search to prove your innocence*
11. *All Insiders will be killed on sight*
12. *All Outsiders now have an earlier curfew of 7:30 P.M. anyone caught outside after this will be shot on sight*
13. *Any citizen, no matter the rank, who consults or aids a Fugitive or Insider will be stripped of their rank and marked as a traitor and enemy of Lieu*

"These rules are the only thing that keeps you safe, my dear people. The very core of our nation." With that, the screen vanished. *Two new rules, is it really getting that bad out there?*

Chapter Fourteen

The next few days flew by, as I learned more and more about the life Asher had lived before I met him.

"So, you moved from Australia when you were only five?" I asked as we strolled down the torn-up roads.

"Mmhm, my brothers were five and three, and my only sister at the time was barely two." He smiled in a bittersweet way.

"Do you ever miss them?" I looked at him, trying to understand how someone else could get over the loss of their siblings.

He bit his lip, before responding. "It comes and goes. Some days are harder than others, but you learn to move on."

I nodded, sighing. "I lost my brother…he…" I paused, unsure if I could tell him. They were searching for relatives of Insiders, but if he was going to let all of his walls down, I had to as well. "My brother was *one of them*." I took in a few shaky breaths, remembering it like it was yesterday. His bleeding body mangled and broken from the cuts. The letter clutched in his fist. "He...he finished the job before they could find him."

"Hey, it's okay." Asher put his hand on my shoulder, trying to comfort me. "I know how horrible those memories can be, Tess." He paused as if realizing what he had called me. All I could hear was my dad and my brother calling me the same thing with such love in their tones. The name he had called me right before he died. When he had lied to me for the last time. I narrowed my eyes, remembering all the pain, the sorrow I had overcome.

"It's okay," I smiled, concealing the old scars in the way I had learned over the years. How to maintain the numbness I had built up as a form of protection for myself. I forced myself to meet his gaze, trying to get the final resting look in my brother's glossy eyes out of my head.

"It's just that..." my words trailed off as I considered telling him. "Never mind." I wasn't ready to let down that particular wall in my life. Not yet.

...

My thoughts wouldn't stay still for a second, and I struggled to fall asleep because of it. Mary had made me as comfortable as she could, but I still couldn't manage to relax.

She had been an Opulent, and she just gave it all away? Hadn't her husband been made an Opulent as well?

After many useless attempts at sleep, I decided to go onto the front porch to clear my head. The air wasn't so bad now that I was used to it, and I just really needed to think.

To my surprise, I found Asher sitting on the step. He hadn't noticed me yet, and I debated going back inside, but then I noticed his cloud. It was a very dark bluish gray, making me smile. It seemed his mother gave him a sense of peace that no one else could.

"Couldn't sleep?" I asked, sitting beside him.

He looked up at me, not even fazed that I was awake at this hour, too. "Even on a good night, I hardly ever sleep." He mumbled in reply. "The house is too confining, it cages you in."

"Are you claustrophobic?" I leaned on my hand, studying his face.

"Something like that." He whispered, seeming lost in an entirely different world of his own.

I sighed, deciding to change the subject. "It's so beautiful here at night." I looked up at the night sky with all of its constellations.

He chuckled a little to himself, "I suppose you of all people would appreciate something as confusing as the sky."

I raised an eyebrow, "What's so confusing about it?"

He shrugged, looking more relaxed than I had ever seen him. "The stars, they all look the same."

"They do not!" I said, very much offended. "There are all sorts of differences."

"Like?" He smiled, clearly amused.

"Mass, size, temperature. Oh! They're even different colors!" I piped up, smiling. It was nice to talk about something I was so passionate about.

"They all look the same to me," he squinted up at the stars, giving me a mock pouty look.

"The hottest and biggest stars are blue and bright, and the coolest and smaller stars are red and dim. Oh, and see that one? The bright one over there?" I pointed, trying to help him see.

"Yeah, what about it?" He leaned back on his elbows.

"That is the North Star, also known as Polaris." I smiled. "It's the one star that never seems to move, one that you can always see, it brings people home. No matter how lost you are, it will always guide you home." Out of the corner of my eye, I noticed him looking at me with a small smile on his face. The sound of his deep breaths coming so close to me was very distracting and I found myself stumbling over words. "It sits directly over the North Pole." I stammered, trying to refocus on my mother's words. "It's kind of nice to think about...having something that will always bring you back, something to always fall back on."

"Someone always waiting for you." He muttered, biting his lip. I looked over at him, surprised to find how close he was to me.

"Someone who understands the memories." I smiled, remembering our conversation earlier.

"You seem so happy," I whispered, my gaze flickering to the dark cloud above him. "So why do you seem so lost?" I looked back into his eyes, for the first time seeing the person behind the colors.

He let out a deep breath, and I felt the warm air blow against a soft patch on my neck. Gently taking my hand in his as if he was scared that he would somehow break me, he spoke quietly, "Because I don't have a North Star to guide me."

"I could be your North Star." I murmured softly, leaning in closer to him. "I could bring you home no matter how lost you get." I found myself looking at his lips, and I could tell he was doing the same.

His eyes fluttered shut. "I'd like that," he breathed, closing the distance between us.

I had imagined a thousand first kisses in my life, but none of them compared to this. He had one hand cupping my cheek, delicately holding me to him, and the other clutching my own. There was something beautiful about the tentativeness of it as if he thought he might somehow shatter the moment. His lips were freezing, but that somehow made it all the more magical. Too soon, he pulled away, leaving me slightly gasping for air.

I smiled, noticing a delicate treble clef forming under his left ear. The symbol for Standards, I wondered if mine was anywhere close to as beautiful as his was.

I looked into his eyes, noticing that they looked brighter somehow, then I noticed his cloud. It was a deep red, the shade found in bright sunsets.

In that one touch, in those small words we had exchanged in these past weeks. I realized I wanted to be the person he fell back onto when he was weak, I wanted to be his guide, his home. Tears filled my eyes as I took in the bright green of his. I had sworn never to feel them again, but I liked these tears.

His eyes were radiant in the moonlight; I had failed to notice it before because I couldn't see past his cloud. But now as I saw him through not the light of his cloud, but through the light of the person behind those colors; I realized I wanted to be his Tess, not because of the society and our songs. Not because of anyone, or anything, but because of the person behind the songs, the person behind the colors. I smiled as that feeling flooded through me so clearly, overwhelmed by joy. I wanted to tell him, but I was scared. If I put those words out there, I could never take them back, and it would hurt a million times more if he left. I was terrified, but I was done missing so many opportunities out of fear.

"Asher," I paused, wondering if I'd regret these words tomorrow. "I…" I looked into his eyes, searching for some sign of doubt, some sign of regret. But all I saw was the same fear I was feeling, to put ourselves that far out there.

"Don't," his eyes flickered to my cheek for some reason. He looked me straight into my eyes. "Don't say it please," he whispered as a bleak expression flickered across his face, but it was gone as fast as it had come. Taken aback, I blinked, feeling offended. What did he mean?

"There's something you need to know, Tess." I took his hand, squeezing it; he was as scared as I was. "I'm-" he was cut off by Mary's voice.

"Oh dear, come inside! You're going to catch a cold," she scolded, with no real anger in her tone.

I smiled at Asher giving him a playful shrug. He gave me a weak smile in return looking like he was going to be sick.

Chapter Fifteen

The next day, I went home despite how much I wanted to stay. I had found a family in Asher and Mary. They seemed to have so little, yet still managed to see the good in everything. As I walked the streets I had gotten so used to seeing, a pang of sadness hit me. How long would this place last? With all of these rules would these streets ever be walked again?

I turned the corner and arrived back on the streets of my neighborhood. I was surprised at how much I was going to miss seeing Asher and his mother every day. Even if the town was run down, and the air conditions were horrible, that place felt more like a home than anywhere else I had lived after my dad left.

I unlocked my apartment's door and stepped inside the halls that seemed so foreign to me now. Mary wasn't in the living room or kitchen waiting for me, and Asher. Oh, Asher! I raced into the bathroom, excitement coursing through me. I wondered what the symbol under my ear looked like, was it different for lower-ranked Standards?

Maybe he even took the symbol of Opulent from his mother! I pushed my hair out of the way and blinked in shock. A symbol I had never seen before in black ink like his was marked underneath my left ear. It was a jagged X, which I assumed meant he was a lower-ranked Standard because the symbol for Opulent was a wine glass. It was a little scary looking, I suppose X's just gave off that effect. All the same, I smiled. Everything felt so right when I was with Asher, giving me more faith in Lieu's system than ever. They never make mistakes, therefore I needed to watch out for the Insiders.

I sat on my couch, and just as I was in the middle of doing my homework, a broadcast appeared on my TV. I immediately perked up, eager to hear what they were announcing.

"Greetings citizens of Lieu," the Official began, looking rather grim. "I have very unfortunate news that may concern your safety, but I can assure you that we are doing all that we can to stop this newfound threat. It is with great sorrow that we must inform you of a horrible accident. It seems that a Fugitive has somehow gotten past the brand and the war. How this scoundrel has survived is beyond our knowledge. If you see anyone acting suspicious or giving you any reason to doubt their word, please bring them in for questioning immediately. The Fugitive that has somehow survived, was found guilty for the murder of his father at eight, and served five years of jail time, with three in the war. He escaped at sixteen and was thought to be dead until now. These suspicions come from a picture a Sentinel got of him walking around a Standard neighborhood. His name is Griffin James Chainbreaker and is extremely dangerous, we have reason to believe that he is aiding the Insiders in their rebellion." My heart froze at those words; *that was the writing that had appeared in my book that night.* He kept talking about better security and ways to protect yourself from him, but I had stopped listening. I felt sick to my stomach, *was I somehow a target?* Finally, these words recaught my attention. "Here is the most recent picture of him we have, he is currently twenty-one, and this is him at nineteen." A picture flashed on the screen, and my heart stopped. Staring back at me was a boy that looked identical to Asher. So many emotions played through my head, making me feel dizzy. Everything began to make sense at once. Why he didn't know what having a song meant, how his mother had sung to him, illegally. Why his cloud was jet-black. All those times he flinched; so much frustration flooded through me I didn't even notice the broadcast ending. But as everything finally sunk in, deepening my fury, I lost it when I realized what that ridiculous X on my cheek meant. I was in danger, I had just been branded by a Fugitive! He lied to me! I couldn't even begin to imagine what was going to happen to me. Asher—no Griffin, was a liar, and he had carelessly put my entire world in danger. I was so furious that I left my apartment and trudged to his house. I wasn't even scared to see him again, I had questions and I was getting answers. It didn't matter if he killed me, I was already a dead man walking.

. . .

I knocked on the door, and when no one answered, I threw it open; it didn't matter anymore, nothing mattered anymore. He was sitting at the table, looking terrified, which I found funny considering it was my life that had been ruined.

"So, Griffin Chainbreaker, is it?" I screamed, throwing my hands in the air surging towards him. "Funny, that's not what I was told!" I was so frustrated that I pushed him out of his chair, onto the wooden floor. "I gave you everything, Griffin! I–I trusted you, I let you in!" I shook my head, unable to believe what was happening. "Do you know how hard that was for me to do? Do you know how many people have hurt me? I suppose that doesn't matter to you, does it? I'm a person behind this target! Do you even notice that anymore?" I hoped hearing his own words thrown back at him would hurt him as much as they had once hurt me.

"I– look, I can explain…" He stumbled over his words, backing away from me.

I was done believing a single word he said, "No! I don't need an explanation, *Griffin*." Suddenly, I remembered my book. "Why? Why did you write those things in my book, *Chainbreaker*?"

"I–I…I wanted you to understand." He pleaded, trying to appear less scared than he was. "I wanted someone to understand before I left."

I paused at those words. "Left?" My voice broke, as my violent urges gave way beneath me.

He gulped, giving a small nod. "Tethys, you can see my cloud. You can see the colors. I…I wasn't going to stay for long…but I couldn't leave you…with nothing."

I sighed, shaking my head. "It would have been better than what you did leave me with." I furiously gestured to the mark on my cheek. "What does it look like?"

"What?" He blinked, looking genuinely confused this time, but still scared.

"The brand," I barked. "Show me." He timidly turned around and paused fiddling with the fabric of his shirt. "What have you got to lose, Fugitive?" He flinched and lifted it. I yanked it up, and my breath caught in my chest.

Catching a glimpse of the torn puckered skin, I squeezed my eyes shut. It was unsettling and at first, I forced myself to focus on the small black crescent moon printed on his shoulder, and the three crows running down the back of his neck; I didn't want to see it. I didn't want to see what we had been taught to fear our whole lives. Gulping, I finally looked down.

Stretched across his entire back, layered over years' worth of scars, were rough and jagged brands of all the symbols forming the broken silhouette of a star. The wine glass for Opulent, treble clef for Standards, chains for Outsiders, an eye that could only be for the Insiders, and an X for the Fugitives. The same X that I wore on my cheek. Over the symbols were two huge cuts stretching from each shoulder to each of his sides, forming a much rougher X than the others. But what was the most horrifying were the sharp letters, dripping blood spelling the word: TRAITOR.

I let his shirt fall back down, too terrified to speak. It was smart of them to put it on someone's back, it was almost sure to paralyze them just long enough to get them killed off in the war.

"I…" I couldn't think of what to say. I was still beyond furious, but I was as stuck as he was. "Why?" He looked down, refusing to meet my gaze. "Why would you go as far as to *kill* your own father."

"My father was a horrible man, right from the start he hated me." He scoffed. "He beat and hurt me. He trapped me in so many ways, but he went too far when he started hurting *her*." He paused, a foul expression playing a cross his face. He seemed too disgusted at the words leaving his mouth to continue. "He was nothing but a monster, and he had no right to hurt her."

"Who?" My anger was replaced with fear, as his voice shook. "Who did he hurt?"

He looked up at me, a fire burning in his emerald green eyes. "My mother. She gave him everything, and he threw it all away."

I froze, too scared to speak, too scared to move. "But I thought they were in love…they were soulmates."

"Of course they were, that's why she left the Opulents for him." He mumbled, anger flaring in his bright eyes. "But that's what Outsiders do; they move on. They take whatever is thrown at them. She continued on after his death, living life in the ruins of the Outsider towns. She found my youngest sister, a baby lost among the memories. I only ever saw her once."

"Do you miss her?" I whispered, still keeping my distance.

"Every day," his eyes were blank, the look he always seemed to get when he spoke about his family. "I can only assume she's dead and move on. Just like all of my other siblings."

I remained silent, too bitter to feel pity for him. But too remorseful to push him away completely.

He sighed and ran his hands through his curly black hair in frustration. "I tried to push away from you, Tethys. I didn't want any of this to happen." He looked up at me at last.

I narrowed my eyes, "Well, it did, and there's nothing you can do to stop it now." I crossed my arms. "So what *are* you going to do, *Griffin*?"

He flinched as if hearing his real name made him realize just how real all of this was. "I…I don't know."

I looked around the makeshift house, anger surging through me once more. "Is that all there is left then? You're just going to give up?"

"What else is there for me? I've been on the run since I was *sixteen*, Tethys! I have lived *five* agonizing years in constant fear." His eyes darted to the door as the wind tussled with the leaves. Then quieter, "I just want it to be over, Tethys…I don't want to fight them anymore."

I blinked, seeing the genuine exhaustion in his eyes. He looked so worn out, so torn.

"My mother has already left, I made sure of it." He said firmly.

"So that's it, you're just going to wait here until you get caught and they kill you?" I had hoped that Griffin would have at least some idea of how to get us out of this.

In a movement so little that I almost didn't even notice it, he slid his black gun to me. "Please." He choked out, his voice was strangled and desperate, nothing like the smooth tone he normally had. "If you do it, you will be regarded as a hero. They'd take you back."

"I–" Shock overcame me as I took in the pleading etched in his eyes. What could drive someone to want something so horrible? Flashbacks of my brother's broken body flashed through my mind, the blood on the wood, his glossy eyes. "I can't…Griff, there has to be another way." I pushed the gun back towards him. He remained silent staring at me. The look in his eyes was stone cold, harsher than they had ever been.

"Don't call me that," he whispered, barely audible. His breathing picked up, as if he was remembering something horrible, the pain in his eyes clearer than the morning sky. "Please, don't call me that."

"I'm sorry…it just slipped out," I stumbled, at how distressed he looked. "I didn't know…"

"Now you do…" He murmured; his stare lost in another time. He narrowed his bright eyes, gazing at a spot on the floor.

"I'm sorry…" I whispered, meaning so many things in that apology.

"We're both as good as dead anyway."

"Surely there's something–"

"There's nothing we can do." He breathed, forcing the gun back into his pocket. "We can only hope they make it quick." I watched as his cloud, with the little that it had lightened, turned inky black right before my eyes.

I let my gaze fall to the ground, feeling so helpless it was almost unbearable. I was about to agree to do it when he began quietly singing a song. *Our song.* It was so quiet that I could just barely make out the lyrics. His voice was choked up, but that somehow made it even more beautiful.

I tentatively began to sing along, hearing the words that used to mean something so different to me yet made so much more sense now. When we finished, I took his hand gently in mine.

"We can't just do nothing, Griffin. We can't just sit around and *now,* after everything, give up."

"And what do you suggest we do then?" He whispered, looking even more hopeless than before

"I don't know, but I'm sure the other Outsiders aren't going to appreciate you dragging them all into this." I nudged him, hoping to make him smile.

He remained silent for a bit, biting his lip in concentration. "Outsiders…" He mumbled quietly, furrowing his eyebrows.

"What about them?" I blinked, confused.

"Wait a minute…Outsiders!" He jumped up to his feet, pulling me up with him. "That's it! That's the answer! The Outsiders!"

"I'm not following…" I raised an eyebrow, looking at him in concern. Now, he was acting insane. Great.

"They've been saying it for years, haven't they?" He asked eagerly. "Come on, no time to explain!"

"Oh! Griffin–" He cut me off by grabbing my arm and racing out the front door.

Chapter Sixteen

His plan was crazy at best and there was a slim chance we would survive, but if we did, generations to come would prosper thanks to our sacrifice. The plan was simple really: rally up the ranks and storm the Opulent city. No big deal. Not a horrible plan that will most likely get us killed.

We decided that the Outsiders would be easiest so we started there first. This was Griffin's territory.

"Okay, I'll go first." He looked over, giving me a reassuring smile. "If things get dicey, you'll run before they find you, right?"

I gulped and nodded, feeling a bit sick.

"Hey," he took my hand, and gave it a small squeeze. "This will most likely end horribly, but if it does, look on the bright side. You won't have to go back to school."

"Wow thanks, that really made me feel better." I smacked his hand away, smirking.

"No tests, no stress." And with that, he ran off into the Outsider town.

I sighed, shaking my head, and went to my secure waiting location. It was smaller than I remembered but no less charming. The wall room seemed so much nicer during the day when we weren't hiding from Assassins.

After an hour or so of waiting, I began to grow impatient. What was taking so long? He said it would be quick. Had they brutally killed him and were looking for me? No, Griffin couldn't die. Not to something as simple as that.

As another hour went by, I had had enough. And using all of my willpower, I began the task of trying to get the door open. Griffin had told me that once the door closed, there was no getting it open without undoing a special lock. Whatever. I did the next best thing and began ramming my shoulder into the door. It hurt sure…like a lot, but I was certain that I could get it open eventually.

"Come on!" I yelled angrily at the door after my fifteenth attempt. Right as I was about to try again, I noticed a strange-looking piece of metal lying near the fireplace. I kneeled and picked it up. It was quite possibly the weirdest shape I had ever seen and coated in rust. I almost cut myself on it and had a mini heart attack. That was a close one.

I had never picked a lock, but it was worth a try. Jamming the metal into the lock, I made sure that I wasn't holding it in such a way that I could cut myself. The metal was slippery because of the rust, but after a few attempts, I managed to break the lock. I decided to take the piece of metal with me, just in case.

Quickly pushing open the door, I sprinted out into the streets. No one was there. That's strange.... Everything was quiet as if nothing was happening at all. I walked farther into the town, searching for any signs of life.

"Hello?" I called down the cobbled streets. Where was he? "Asher?" I decided it would be safer to use his fake name. No reply. I continued strolling down the streets, farther and farther into the Outsider town. "Hello?" I called a little louder, feeling frustrated.

"H–hello…?" A small voice responded from somewhere behind me.

I quickly turned, wielding my rusty piece of metal. A little girl stood there wincing, covering her face. I blinked, slowly lowering it. She looked far too young to be out on her own.

"Hey," I held out my free hand. "It's okay." She spread her fingers apart to reveal blue eyes staring timidly back at me. She was shaking, but after a little bit took my hand. She couldn't have been much older than nine years old.

"My name's Tethys," I gave her a warm smile. "What's your name?"

She didn't reply, she simply remained silent, staring at me uncertainly. I took in her appearance sadly; she wore a torn light blue dress covered in soot and dirt. Her white-blond hair was tangled, and she was bleeding from small cuts on her arms and legs. Her cloud was a light blue leaning towards purple, which I had never seen before.

"I promise that I won't hurt you." I smiled, crouching down beside her. "I'm looking for someone."

Her face lit up, "Me too!"

"Maybe I can help you find whoever you're looking for," I suggested, kneeling. She looked familiar, but I wasn't sure why. Maybe it was the hopeful look in her eyes or her facial structure, but I knew I had seen it before. "Who are you looking for?"

She looked down, sniffling. "Bam Bam."

I blinked, slightly taken aback. "Um…okay. Well, I'll help you find 'Bam Bam' if you help me find my friend, okay?"

"Okay." She smiled, looking relieved.

"Do I get to know your name now?" I took her hand, and we began strolling down the streets.

"Sugar." She piped up as she began skipping.

"What a nice name." I couldn't help but smile as she skipped happily beside me.

"How'd you lose your friend?" She asked innocently.

"He ran on ahead, even though I told him to wait." I smiled, patting her head. "How'd you lose 'Bam Bam'?"

"I…" she blinked. "I don't remember."

I decided not to push her and changed the topic. "So, have you seen anyone else walking along these streets? They aren't usually this empty."

"No," she walked on ahead. "They were much fuller yesterday, maybe it has something to do with what happened last night."

"What…what happened last night?" I gulped, fear surging through me.

"*They* came." She looked at me way too seriously for a little girl. "They were looking for something, I don't know what. They kept asking people questions, lots, and lots of questions." She shuddered, "then the shots came. They were loud. I didn't like them."

"I wouldn't either," I mumbled, feeling horrible for her having to go through that. What had our society come to?

Finally, we came across a full town square of people. They were all turned towards someone in the middle, and I let out a breath of relief. They weren't rioting; in fact, they looked hopeful. Sugar looked confused and began tugging on the bottom of my shirt.

"What's going on?" She asked, searching for a way to see over the crowd.

"I don't know yet, why don't we see if we can get a closer view?" I led her through the crowd, trying to get closer to the center. As we pushed past a few more people, I saw his little black curls peeking out above the person in front of me. "Maybe 'Bam Bam' is somewhere in this crowd," I suggested. "Do you want to look?"

She wasn't paying attention to me anymore, instead, she was distracted trying to see over the people in front. "What's going on?"

"Here, I'll try to get us closer." I led Sugar up to a gap in the front and felt immediately relieved as I saw him fully, but Sugar had other plans.

"Bam Bam!" She cheered, sprinting towards Griffin excitedly. I blinked in shock, as he turned toward the name. Many expressions played across his face as he found the source of the noise.

"Sugar?" He looked more surprised than I had ever seen him, and quickly pulled her into a tight hug. I didn't fully understand how she knew him, then it hit me. He had had a younger sister who he had only seen once. The crowd around began cheering, as Griffin fell to his knees, hugging her even tighter. "You're okay!" He cried, pure joy echoing in his tone. My heart melted at the sight of him, forgetting any anger I had held onto. I felt that feeling so plainly in my heart, waiting to be let out.

I cheered along with the crowd; this was what a true society should be like, not separated by wealth, but like one big family. One nation that worked together. The clouds above their heads were all bright yellow. Everyone here, despite how little they had, was happy. I looked over to Griffin's cloud hopefully and smiled seeing it a deep shape of red. Brighter than the morning sky. Not quite yellow, but not remotely close to black.

It seemed as if I was watching an entire nation of people who had next to nothing their entire lives gain more than anything the Opulents ever had.

Chapter Seventeen

One part of our plan was done, and now it was time for the Standards. The very part that I was dreading more than actually invading the Opulent city. This was going to be difficult, but it was my home. I knew that it would be much harder to sway the Standards, or even get them thinking about rebellion. I had been there before, and if I hadn't met Griffin I would still be there. Why would anyone want freedom when they think that they already possess the fullest version of it?

As we approached the entrance to the neighborhoods, my heart began to race in my chest. Not only were we doing something highly illegal, but we were doing it as one of the most wanted Fugitives ever to live, and a war criminal. But even with that thought in mind, I knew exactly where we needed to go first.

As I walked down the familiar streets, I felt as if it wasn't home anymore. I didn't like the feelings this whole experience was giving me. Why did the streets I had walked my entire life seem so stranger?

If you had told me a year ago that I would ever step foot in this house again, I probably would have run. But here I was, preparing to face them for the first time in eight years.

Griffin knocked on the door, and after a few minutes with no answer, knocked again. The door opened a centimeter, and when she saw that it wasn't a Sentinel, she opened it fully.

"Hi, Mrs. Johnson," I waved, reassuringly. "Can we come in?"

Her eyes were locked on Griffin, and I scolded myself. His face had been broadcasted on live TV. She was probably terrified.

Without taking her eyes off of Griffin, she gave us a shaky nod. We walked past her, and as she closed the door behind us, she opened her mouth to speak before quickly shutting it again.

"Have you heard anything about…you know?" I asked, cautiously.

She didn't look sad or like she even fully heard me as she shook her head.

"You survived." She whispered in awe, her gaze locked on Griffin. "Did you know a little boy named Drew?"

He looked very uncomfortable, which I didn't quite get. "I– how young was he?"

"Around eleven." She said eagerly. "Dirty blond hair, freckles, dark brown eyes." She looked so hopeful at this point. I couldn't help but smile as her cloud turned a bright hopeful shade of orange.

Griffin's next expression was stony and guarded. "He fought on the front lines beside me…he…he didn't even last a week."

Her expression fell, and she managed to give us a grim nod. "Thank you."

"I'm sorry…" He mumbled awkwardly.

A hard silence fell; I wasn't sure how to open the conversation we came here for without seeming rude.

Griffin cleared his throat, trying to get through this quickly. "Mrs. Johnson, we're not here to hurt you or force you into anything, but we do have an offer to make."

She gulped but nodded for him to continue. I didn't blame her for being uneasy, Griffin wasn't the most comforting sight in the world.

"I understand that you lost your son to the Opulents," he continued, softening his tone. "So we thought you might want to hear this."

I gave him a reassuring nod, "We're done listening to the unfair laws of the Opulents, Mrs. Johnson. We're rising up, and we want you to join us."

"How will you ever win?" She asked, not seeming exactly opposed, just concerned.

"We already have the Outsiders, who outnumber them ten to one," Griffin interjected rather proudly. "And also, we know how to fight, and what it means to struggle."

I nudged him, silently trying to send him the message that, "*the standards don't know how to fight either.*" He raised an eyebrow at me, then continued.

"You can join us, or remain living in fear." He said finally. I smacked his arm underneath the table for putting it so harshly. She was a more sensitive case. In response, he grabbed my wrist, preventing me from hitting him again.

"Say no more," she said, looking hopeful. "I'm in."

Griffin gave me a triumphant look and snuck a kiss on my hand. Then turning back towards her said, "Congratulations, you've joined the revolution. Meet us at the entrance to the Opulent town early on Friday morning."

Chapter Eighteen

We made sure to leave her house at differing times, as not to raise suspicion. Then we met up again in a side alley, besides our next house.

"What was all that for?" He asked, jogging up to me.

"The subtle under-the-table fight?" I asked, rolling my eyes.

"Yeah, what the heck? I was doing great." He pouted.

"We agreed that we would make this as much of a light choice as possible." I sighed.

"Look, Tess. This isn't light." I didn't know why he was so defensive about it. "This is the future! Something so many people would kill for!" He groaned. Then in a softer tone, "this is *our* future." He took my hand, with a pleading look in his eyes.

I looked away; *he was unbelievable sometimes. Did he honestly believe that after everything, all of the lies? I'd just take him back? Did he think there was still a chance for us to be an us? Did I still think there was?*

I felt his chilly fingers let go of mine and cup my chin, asking—not forcing me—to look up at him.

"Hey," he smiled. "I'm sorry, I'm just not the best at this." I looked into his bright green eyes, letting out an exhale. I could tell he meant it, though I didn't understand why his tone implied something much deeper than just simply messing up our speech.

"Let's just move on," I said turning away and heading up the steps of the house. I was excited to see her again, and if the circumstances were any different, I might have just burst in without knocking, but they were. We had business to do. I rapped a few times on the door before my mom quickly pulled it open. She didn't even seem to register that Griffin was there.

"Oh, Tethys!" She pulled me into a very tight embrace, tears instantly springing to her eyes. "You weren't answering my calls, and I was so worried– Oh! I'm so glad you're safe!" She held me if possible, even tighter, making it hard to breathe. I hadn't realized how tense I had been until I finally felt safe in my mother's arms once more. I held her back, feeling so many things at once. Relief, safe, home. I finally felt like I was home. These streets didn't feel so cold anymore.

My mom suddenly pulled away and pushed me behind her with such force I almost tumbled over. "Get away from my daughter, and my house." She hissed, pulling out her phone.

"No, mom," I mumbled, realizing Griffin had just been standing there that whole time. "It's okay, he's with me."

Her mouth dropped open, looking from me to him. "You…he…I…what?"

"Long story. Let's go inside."

Chapter Nineteen

After a series of very awkward introductions, and a speed round of getting to know you, we were all caught up…well, mostly. I left out the story about the X on my cheek.

"We are taking a stand for what's right." I nodded, feeling confident in our point.

"Honey, they are only doing what's best for you." She insisted, shaking her head.

"People dying is what's best then?" Griffin snapped, making me nudge him to stop 'helping'.

"They are monsters." My mom scowled.

"Hyperion wasn't a monster, mom." I blurted, unable to stop the words from escaping my mouth. I hadn't said his name in so many years, and the name felt strange. A pang of unexpected sadness caught me off guard. My mother's expression changed to something bitter, but she remained silent. "He never hurt anyone," I said, regretting even bringing him up. "He was…he was so kind." I let my gaze drop as she did the same.

"He was a dangerous accident," She insisted, not sounding very sure. "The Officials said so."

"Maybe they aren't right," I screamed, losing patience.

She looked taken aback, "Of course they're right, sweetie. They always are."

"They paired us together," I pointed out, getting my temper back in check. "Were they right about that?"

"Paired? I–but that's impossible…he's a Fugitive." She shook her head, looking from Griffin to me.

"The Chanteuses have messed up before," I sighed.

"Many times," Griffin added.

"Tethys, I just don't know." As she spoke, she kept her gaze locked on him. "What you are suggesting is just ridiculous! I have no choice but to assume that he has somehow gotten into that head of yours, I mean seriously! Take on the Officials? Why? They have done nothing but good for us, for…for everyone!" She stumbled over her words, inching away from Griffin.

"Mom, that's just what we've been told to believe!" I was beginning to feel frustrated, but I quickly composed myself.

"Tethys, you know the rules." She said, looking suddenly solemn. "You've heard rule number thirteen."

Slowly, she pulled out a smooth gun with such shaky hands, I could barely register what she meant.

"Mom?" I blinked in horror as she aimed it right at my heart. What was happening?

"I'm so sorry," she whispered, closing her eyes. I looked up at the stark gray cloud above her head, a solemn, foreboding shade. "But it's for the greater good of the society."

Before I could even react, Griffin was in front of me holding his own gun protectively over me. "There will be no need for that." He snapped coldly, covering me from her.

"You have betrayed Lieu," She said again, but this time firmer, still tightly clutching onto the gun. "My loyalty is to my nation."

He turned to look at me with regretful eyes and mouthed 'I'm so sorry'. As I fully processed what he meant, all I could do was nod before the bullet sunk right into her heart.

Chapter Twenty

The world seemed to go silent around me; my screams were drowned out by the sound of the gunshot. My mother's limp body fell to the floor, dead in seconds. Her once bright cloud vanishing right before my eyes. I couldn't even fight back as Griffin carried my struggling body out of the house. She was gone. My mother was gone. Griffin had killed her…my mother had been going to kill me…I had told him to do it…

I didn't know what was true anymore. Everything seemed like a lie, like something just being fed to me to keep me quiet. Who was I? I wasn't a murderer, this wasn't supposed to be a murder mission. She was supposed to join…she was supposed to stand with me.

As my world crumbled around me, I realized that I was alone, the one person I had always relied on, was gone. The one constant in my life. The only person who had never hurt me was gone. She had been going to hurt me though…but even then, why did it have to end like this? Would they bury her body? Suddenly all of the struggle left my body, there was nothing left, no one I was still fighting for.

Reaching an empty alley, Griffin set me down against the wall. Blood splattered his pale face…my mother's blood…I desperately tried to break away from him; he was a murderer.

"Tethys, stop!" He urged, hushing me.

"You killed her!" I screeched, clawing his arms. "You killed her, you monster!" As my gaze fell, I noticed colorful and intricate designs weaving together on his arm. The ink swirling and curving to form delicate puzzles pieces. I hadn't ever noticed them before. It was beautiful in a twisted way. It was something that held meaning and I wanted to destroy it. I wanted to see the art ruined. The once beautiful canvas splattered in blood just like my mother's body. I saw the scrapes on his arms begin to bleed, and I dug in deeper. I wanted him to feel the pain my mother had felt. The pain he had stopped me from feeling. I pulled my hands away, tears threatening to spill down my cheeks. Who had I become?

As we heard a noise coming near, he clapped his hand over my mouth. I struggled, wanting them to find us. To find him. To find me.

When the footsteps faded away completely, he removed his hand. The hand that had taken my mother's life. The hand that had taken my lifeline from me. Yet, the hand that had saved *my* life.

"I hate you," I whispered, unable to process that the words had even escaped my mouth. "I hate you, Griffin Chainbreaker."

"She was going to kill you, Tethys." He looked into my teary eyes, trying to keep me still. "She was going to do the same to you in cold blood."

"I hate you!" I screamed, my voice sounding lost in my ears. Who did I hate? I didn't even know if I was talking to him anymore. Why was I saying this?

"You don't mean that." He whispered, patient as ever.

"Yes, I do." I tried to escape his grip on me again, but this time he was holding me down.

"Stop! Just stop, Tethys!" He yelled, finally losing hold of his temper. "People die, they all fade away. No one stays! Ever!" There was a pang of sadness in his tone, that I didn't quite get. "Some people die way too young, some people live until they are old and content, but they all die eventually." Then softer, "some little boys get sent to war to die. Innocent little boys. Some people who just aren't taught how to survive." Tears began to trickle down his bloody face, smearing the deep crimson painted on his milky skin. "Some people die even if they weren't supposed to. Even if they did nothing wrong!" *Drew.* The word hung in the air; he didn't say it. He didn't have to. "I held him as he died, watching the smoke reduce to nothing but ashes." He heaved at his last words, finally losing control. The chains binding him, finally snapped. He was sobbing.

I stared at him awestruck. I had never seen him cry, not like this. These were sobs that wracked his entire body. Sobs that held so much pain that they hurt to watch. Griffin had been treading on a thin sheet of ice, and he had just fallen into the icy waters below.

I sat there speechless, grief-stricken, unsure of where to go or what to do. I was so furious that I didn't even know who I was mad at anymore. Griffin, the society, the Officials, me. I was just mad at the world! For how unfair it is, for how many people had to leave me. I had no more family left, first my dad, then my brother, and now…now my mother. For once I had no one to fall back onto, no one left in my safety bubble. No one left whose clouds were never supposed to go dark.

After a moment of silence, he spoke again. Softly, his voice cracking from the tears, "We tried doing it your way, now we're doing it my way."

"No," I whispered, my voice barely audible over the gentle trickle of rain. "There has to be another way."

The musical pitter patter of raindrops across the alley felt wrong. Didn't the world know what had happened? Shouldn't it be grieving? His face looked eerie in the poorly lit alley, making the crimson blood splatters too red. Too bright.

"This is the rebellion," he announced, much louder than he was speaking before. His eyes were red, and his voice was rubbed raw. "And you have two choices: join us or die."

Chapter Twenty-One

I watched as he marched out of the dark alley, instructing me to meet him in the center of the Standard town bright and early the following morning. I didn't know where to go, certainly not to my mother's house.

As I trudged the familiar path back to my apartment, I thought over everything that had happened. Surely there was another way, a way that ensured no more dead. But there wasn't, we were doing what the Officials had done to us for countless years.

That night, I had nightmare after nightmare. The images of my mother, father, and brother's broken bleeding bodies filled my dreams.

After hours of attempting to sleep, I decided it was useless. I couldn't bear to see them like this anymore. I walked over to my record book and flipped to the pictures of lives lost in the war. I found my father's face first, I hadn't looked at him in years. It had hurt way too much. I found a boy that could only have been Drew, he looked just as I had remembered him. Small, scared, and hopeless. Beside his picture I found Griffin's; they had clearly tried to deny him surviving the war for quite a while.

I wondered if the Sentinels had found my mother's body yet; I didn't know if it would be better or worse if they had.

When the sun finally began to rise over the big, grassy hills of the field, I started the journey to the town square. I didn't know what Griffin planned to do, but I knew it wouldn't be peaceful. Then again, this *was* the only way left. Even with that thought, I felt sick as I walked the path to the center. No one was here yet, so I waited trying not to raise any suspicion.

An hour went by and I began to question my timing when I saw them. An entire force of Outsiders, yelling and shouting to the people in the houses. Some broke down doors if they didn't leave, others came out of their houses willingly. I watched in horror as entire houses went up in flames. I saw a woman standing on the roof of her own house shouting. I couldn't make out her words, so I risked getting closer.

Upon closer inspection, I recognized her face. A woman named Miss García, who had run the ice cream shop for countless years. She had streaks of what looked like blood at first, but to my great relief was only red paint, forming swirls across her face.

"I won't sing for you anymore, Officials!" She screamed, with a hysterical laugh. "It's about time!"

I watched her shout, and cheer on the Outsiders in confusion. Harmless Miss García with war paint drawn on her face? Yelling for the rebellion? It didn't make sense until I realized what she meant about the songs. She said her soulmate had died before she could find him, a genius cover-up for being an Insider.

"Tethys!" I turned as I heard my name. Griffin was jogging up to me through the crowd. He had three streaks of black war paint going through his right eye, resembling the scars on his face, mockingly. "Do you see this?" He asked, looking around at the cheering people.

"I see houses going up in flames." I crossed my arms, as Miss García ran past me screaming. This was exactly how people like my mother got killed. Innocent, brainwashed people.

"That's not what I'm referring to," he rolled his eyes. "Do you see the hope? Tethys, the Outsiders haven't been hopeful since before the ranks were invented!"

I looked around and couldn't deny the clear relief and joy I saw. Until now, I had never seen the quiet little ice cream lady raise her voice above even a whisper. But I also saw the burning houses, the Standards screaming. I could have been in their situation if I hadn't met Griffin.

"Give them a choice, please." I pleaded, turning back to him. "Don't let them take their lives, they don't know what they're doing. They follow the Opulents blindly."

Griffin looked at my distressed face, and nodded, taking my hands. "Okay, I'll tell the Outsiders to leave the killing to the Sentinels."

As dark as that sentence was, relief flooded through me. Griffin wasn't a cold-blooded murderer, he wanted as many people as possible to live too. I didn't know who to blame for my mother's death, but I couldn't keep hating him relentlessly for it. Not if the cause was to save my own life in the end. That strange feeling that I always seemed to get around him flooded through me again, and I realized I couldn't hate him. Not fully anyway. Especially not when I had played a role in her death as well.

"Thank you," I whispered, giving his hand a small kiss, just like he had done in Mrs. Johnson's house.

He smiled, looking a little more hopeful. "Now, shall we begin the destruction of the nation of Lieu?"

I rolled my eyes, "Sure thing, but only if we can name it the nation of Tess after."

Griffin looked me up and down, "Yeah right." He turned to leave, but I gently grabbed his arm, noticing the claw marks I had placed in my anger.

"I'm sorry," I whispered, taking in the destruction I had caused. The beautiful tattoo stained with the crimson that *I* had put there. None of this was his fault; I would have been dead if she was still alive.

"I've been hurt before, it's okay." A sad expression played across his face. "I can take it."

I cupped his cheeks, gently massaging the scar beneath. He seemed to relax under the warmth of my hands, encouraged by the comforting touch. I couldn't ever fully forget my mother, but she was gone, there was no changing that. So what was stopping me from being with him? Nothing, but my fears. He needed someone to love him just as much as I did; then came that feeling so strong in me again. I kissed him gently, the scar on his cold lip felt rough against mine. "Now, let's go take down the Opulents!"

Chapter Twenty-Two

The responses from the Standards were varied, but in the end, we had almost the entire town with us. Those who didn't join us had dark ends…ends I didn't want to speak of. Even though we let them live, some thought that if the nation fell, they should too. Was that what I would have thought? Was that the end I would have met? I shook the thoughts from my head as I crawled into bed that night. A day, that was how much time we had left until taking on the central city. I didn't know how Friday morning would go, but I was starting to feel anxious. I decided to attempt some of my homework, but I just couldn't focus. If anything, it made me feel even more clueless.

Except for the light trickle of rain outside, it was completely silent. Too quiet. As I threw my notebook across the room in frustration, a knock came at my front door, startling me. Who would come knocking at this hour?

I slowly got up, pulling on a sweatshirt, and walked cautiously to my door. I took a peek through the tiny hole, and relief flooded through me as I recognized the face outside.

After opening it and letting him in, I quickly shut the door and locked it. Griffin pulled down his hood, panting a little.

"Oh, thank goodness," he breathed, pulling me into a tight hug. "You're okay."

I blinked in confusion, holding him just as close regardless. "Why wouldn't I be?"

"I thought they might have gotten to you." He quickly explained, looking extremely distraught.

"Who? The Sentinels?" I asked, pulling away.

He nodded his head towards my room, peeking out my door again. "Let's talk in there, too many ears around."

After I was seated on my bed, he began pacing and explained.

"Gone? How?" I blinked, taking his hand. Where could Sugar have gone? She was only nine…it didn't make sense.

"I don't know," he said, clearly more upset than he was showing. He pulled out of my grip, running his hands through his curly black hair in frustration. "I came back to our promised meeting place, and she was gone." He buried his head in his hands. "What if they got to her?" He spoke softly, his voice barely audible over the rain falling outside.

"Hey, Griffin." I stood up, pulling him into another embrace. "It's okay, she's smart. She was on her own for a while before," I pointed out. "She probably sensed that something was wrong and ran."

"The whole place was turned upside down," he whispered, his eyes blank. "Every drawer opened, dishes were shattered, doors burned down to the ground."

"They were clearly looking for something, meaning they might not have found her," I reassured him, though I wasn't sure I believed it myself. When the Opulents wanted something, they stopped at nothing until they got it.

Griffin looked into my eyes, searching for answers. "Maybe." He let his gaze fall to the ground, swallowing hard.

"Griffin, look at me." I gently lifted his chin, meeting his blank stare. "This isn't your fault."

He buried his head in his hands again, unable to meet my gaze. "If I had just brought her with me–"

"To the whole rebellion thing? She definitely would have been hurt," I pointed out. "You did everything you could."

"I lost her again, after finally being reunited…Tess, I...I don't know what to do." He looked so lost, so helpless.

"Hey." I gently led him over to my bed, sitting beside him. "Maybe Mary came back to take her with her?"

"Surely she would have told me," Griffin insisted, reluctantly letting me hold him.

I ran my fingers through his hair. "How could she? If she left a note, the Sentinels would have found it."

"They've already taken so much from me," he whispered, snapping into that distant stare he always seemed to get trapped in. "What's stopping them from taking her too?"

"They haven't taken everything, and even if they did…" I gulped, unable to imagine a future without Sugar's tiny smile. "Even if they did find her, your mother is still safe." He curled up beside my chest, not looking reassured in the slightest.

"And you're still here," he whispered after a few moments of silence. "I still have you."

"You always will," I kissed the top of his head, remembering that night under the stars. It seemed so long ago now.

"Don't do that," he muttered, looking up at me with those bright green eyes that always rendered me speechless. "Don't make promises that you can't keep. Don't give me hope."

I pulled away facing him, wanting to let that feeling out so badly. *If I say those three words, there is no taking them back.* "Griffin, I need to know that if I jump, you'll be on the other side. Please, just tell me you'll be waiting to catch me."

He paused, pulling away from me a little. "I...I can't, Tess." He was looking blankly at a spot in the room, years and years of horror reflecting in his tired eyes. He had used the word trapped after the broadcast that seemed so far away now. Caged, confined. Suddenly so many things made sense. Pushing me away, the guarded looks. He was terrified of commitment, of putting himself into something and not being able to pull out. Of being trapped. And then I realized something else, the chains that always seemed to hold him back, the cold, distant glances. He trapped himself. More than anyone else, it was him. The iron cage that always surrounded him, confined his every breath; the bars he feared beyond hope, beyond all reason, he had constructed himself.

"It's okay," I whispered, wanting to leave him with no doubt of who I was. "I'll wait. I won't leave." Flashbacks of my father caught me off guard, making me realize just how similar our situations were. So many people gone, such little trust left.

He looked at me, looking like he wanted to say something, but whether he had wanted to or not, I would never know. A huge broadcast appeared in front of us.

"Attention citizens of Lieu," the Head Official, Mr. Lieu began, sounding less confident than usual. "There have been disturbances in our ranks, and you and your loved ones may be in danger. You are not to leave your house unless absolutely necessary. I assure you we are doing everything in our power to stop these riots. It seems the Fissure War is not our most dangerous threat anymore. Some people seem to think that our system is wrong." He actually laughed at that. "We decided to remind them of who we are, and how much we have fought to get here today. Henry la Beaulieu did not fight among so many others to form our wonderful nation, only to see it fall at the hands of some uneducated, filthy criminals."

The screen panned out to reveal a giant stage beside his podium, and on the stage stood Sugar, trembling and beaten.

The cloud above her head was a shade of purple I had only seen once. Right before they had taken Drew.

"NO!" Griffin screeched, jumping to his feet. "Sugar!" His screams were lost in the cheering crowd of Opulents. How heartless could they be? She was only a little girl! I was yelling with him, trying to reach Sugar through the screen. It was useless, but it was the only thing we could do, the only way to reach her for what may be the last time.

"Take this as a message, rebels. Stop this rebellion." He paused as the camera dramatically zoomed in on Sugar's tiny, trembling form. She was crying, smudging the dirt and blood that stained her precious face. "Or die."

"Sugar!" Griffin fell to his knees, his voice cracking from the strain of tears.

She called out for a Bam Bam that would never come right before the bullets pierced her body.

Chapter Twenty-Three

The rest of Mr. Lieu's words were lost in the sounds of our screams. Another gone, another dead. She had been so young. My thoughts went to Drew, a boy I had barely known yet understood so much about now. This society was so broken, so corrupt. How had I ever trusted these people? They took my family! They took Sugar!

Time passed by without us. I was overwhelmed with grief; so many questions went unanswered. The only thing I still knew to be true was the horrible sting of reality, the knowledge that they were never coming back. He was crying, I had never seen him cry like this. Harder than when he lost all hope that day. Because he hadn't lost all hope then, not as he had now.

Half-blind by my tears, I stumbled over to the place where Griffin had fallen. When I got close enough, he wordlessly pulled me into a hug, burying his face in my shoulder. I dug my hands into his hair, doing the same. I could feel the fabric of my shirt quickly become wet with tears, and I was sure his was too. I didn't know who was holding on tighter, but in that one small moment, it hit me. *He* was the only person I had left now. My final lifeline, my only support beam. And I was his.

My tears began to fall more rapidly. "Griffin, I'm sorry! I'm so, so—"

"Shhhh," he urged, kissing my neck gently. "It's not your fault, you don't need to apologize to me."

"I gave you hope, even though you told me not to!" I insisted, guilt finally piling onto me. "I–I hurt you—"

"A lot of people have hurt me, Tess." He pulled away, looking into my teary eyes. "But not you."

I studied his gentle eyes, running my hands down his scarred arms. I remembered the first time I had seen his eyes in the dark of my room, it seemed like a lifetime ago. Back then they had seemed so cold, so unforgiving, nothing like the gentle, tired eyes looking back at me now. I felt as if I was seeing him for the first time all over again. Not as Asher, not as another cloud gone dark, not as a Fugitive, but as Griffin. Someone who had been through so much, had everything taken away from him but continued to give back. Someone who had seen so much death in his life, that he almost lost himself among them.

"Griffin, you've been strong for so long," I whispered, feeling hot tears of my own, dripping down my cheeks. "It's okay to be weak."

He let out a shaky breath, wearing a mixed expression. He mouthed something, seeming lost in that world of his again. I feared one day, I'd lose him for good. That he'd get so far lost in his past, that I would never be able to reach him again. And I thought I had when he spoke. Softly, with a gentle smile curving his lips. "Griff," he whispered. "Call me Griff. I love the way you say it."

I cupped his scarred cheek in my hand, wiping away the tears. "I love you, Griff." I pressed my lips to his, giving him the whisper of a kiss. "And I know that you aren't ready, but I'll wait. I won't leave. Whatever happens tomorrow, I want to leave you with no doubt in your head of that."

When he smiled, his green eyes seemed brighter somehow, and I didn't realize why until I looked up. The cloud that had once been black, hopeless, and empty, was now a radiant yellow. Brighter than the sun, casting light upon his features in a whole new way. Even though my vision began to blur with the tears filling my eyes, there was no mistaking how bright that broken cloud had become.

Slowly, as if he was afraid that he might shatter me, he took me in his arms and gave me a shaky kiss. He began softly singing the chorus of our song, his voice choked up with tears. I joined, wiping them away. I felt as if this sweet harmony was in dedication to Sugar. She would not be forgotten, and neither would…neither would my mother.

Chapter Twenty-Four

Friday morning was etching closer as the hours ticked by. I needed more time; more time to think, more time to face the truth. I hadn't slept at all, instead, I had spent the fading night calculating every single place I had gone wrong in my life to get me here. So many moments, so many words I wished that I could take back. Where were my friends now? What had happened after I had cut them all off. For what? Because my brother had made a mistake that cost the people around him more than he would ever know? What would have happened if I had just stuck with my mom? Just ignored my soulmate and had given up? No. There were a lot of things I regretted, but Griffin was not one of them. No matter how much had happened to get us here, I would never trade the boy curled up beside me for anything. That scared me. The only people I had ever cared about like this were dead; I had never been willing to give my life for anyone, yet for Griffin, I'd do it in a heartbeat.

What would have happened if I had pulled the trigger? I shuddered remembering the look in his eyes and scooted closer to him. He wasn't asleep, and I could tell by his ragged breaths that he was still crying. I wished that I could have turned back time. I wished that I could have gone back to the days when my brother was alive, when life was easier. How did I get here? How had they all died?

Thoughts ran rampant as I stared blankly at my bedroom's wall. What if today was the day that I died? I didn't want to die...even if it meant seeing *them* again. Feeling completely numb was a strange sensation, it made the world seem darker, harsher.

Calloused, cold fingers found their way to mine, making me smile. I squeezed his hand, gently stroking his hair away from his forehead.

"We're going to make it...you know that, right?" he murmured softly into my shoulder. "No matter what happens later, we'll still be alright."

"Don't make promises that you can't keep," I whispered, meeting his tired gaze.

He gave me a thin smile. "Tess, I need you to promise me something." He paused, letting his gaze fall to our intertwined fingers. "Whether we win or lose tomorrow; no matter how many others around us fall...I need you to live. I can't lose you too."

I gently lifted his chin, to look at me. "I promise." He smiled, giving me a delicate kiss.

"Thank you," he breathed.

"And Griff?" I felt a smile forming.

"Yes?"

"That goes for you too. I can't go losing you either." I gave him a gentle nudge.

He took my hand and gave it a light kiss. "You won't, Tess." Then looking back up at me, he grinned, "Ready for whatever comes next?"

"Ready for whatever comes next." I gave his hand a gentle squeeze. "Now, let's go show the Opulents just how 'wonderful' our nation really is."

. . .

I'd only ever seen the Opulent streets before in broadcasts. They were huge and so shiny that I could see my reflection in the polished, marble tiles. As we passed the enormous golden gates, I expected to see some citizens wandering around opening shops, but the town was completely desolate. The sun peeked over the mountains, causing the gold of the head building's roof to sparkle. The world outside these gates started at eight o clock; I guessed the Opulents didn't have school or work to go to seeing how they had private tutors and no need for extra money.

Groups of Outsiders and Standards silently flooded in around the stage, waiting for the signal to strike. Seeing two polar opposite groups of people uniting was strange. The Standards with their perfect postures, and neat clothing beside hunched over Outsiders with grime coating their scarred faces. There was a clear divide between them.

We made our way to the stage where most of the broadcasts took place, where they had killed Sugar. Her blood had once stained these tiles. I bitterly looked down at the white stones; how many innocent people had died here?

Griffin's hand found its way to mine and grabbed it. I met his gaze and gratefully squeezed it, remembering the broadcast in vivid detail. This was for her.

He gave me a grim nod, pulling up his mask. I followed suit, creeping into position around the stage. It was crucial that we were completely silent until the explosives went off. One of the Outsiders, a man named Liam, had wired them the night before, he explained that when they attacked the old towns some of the explosives hadn't gone off and they had rewired them. It was a mystery to me how he had even known how to do that.

After what couldn't have been longer than half an hour, Griffin held up two fingers. The message was clear: *two minutes*. Anxious waves were bubbling inside of me, making me feel sick. I silently pushed myself closer to Griffin, keeping my eyes locked on the podium. He wordlessly laced his rough fingers in mine.

Holding up a one in the air, he leaned over and pressed his lips to my ear, "Be careful."

I gulped, nodding as he pulled away with a solemn look. I hadn't ever seen an explosion before, and I hoped it wouldn't be too loud. Would it be close enough to harm us? No, they would have thought of that…right?

Without warning, the podium in front of us erupted in flames, sending waves of boiling hot air towards us. I was thrown into Griffin by the impact, who protectively pulled his arm around me and started barking out orders. A rush of giddy excitement coursed through me; we blew up the stage! I helped blow up an Opulent landmark!

Jumping to my feet, I surged forward along with the others. This was it, we were doing it. Sentinels and Officials flooded towards us, but they were all still too disoriented from the explosion to properly fight. We pushed through their forces like it was nothing, but I knew they would come to their senses soon. The explosion had paved a way for us, but it hadn't taken out nearly as many Sentinels as it should have. All the smoke from the fire made it hard to breathe and stung my lungs. Opulent citizens were stumbling out of their grand houses around us, clearly confused.

The Officials screamed at the citizens to get back to their houses, but there was too much noise for anyone to take notice. People were screeching, and even crying. I would have felt bad if these weren't the very people who had cheered for Sugar's death.

Bitterly, I continued forward. We were a force, marching towards the head building. The Officials were outnumbered.

"We're going to make it!" Griffin called excitedly from behind me. I turned back to face him, smiling. "I told you, silly."

I sighed, beginning to jog towards him when the building to my right burst into flames with an ear-rattling boom. I was knocked to the ground by the force, and quickly stumbled up trying to get to Griffin. I sprinted towards him, horrified. Fire shot through my arm, feeling like it was burning. The Assassins. They were everywhere, surrounding us. I stumbled blindly towards him, the pain becoming unbearable. My vision turned black at the edges as it doubled. *I am dying. I am dying.* I didn't want to die.

"Tethys!" His voice echoed over the shouting, as his desperate eyes searched through the crowd. My ears were ringing, and everything sounded muffled as if my head was underwater. I tried to call after him, but the words were replaced with a strangled scream as someone grabbed my injured arm. I turned, looking straight into the eyes of the Sentinel who had taken my brother.

"Runs in the family, huh?" He said with a smirk. I tried to rip my hurt arm out of his grip, but it only made the bleeding worse. My vision was going blurry around me; the pain was blinding. "What's wrong, child? Don't have a song?" He asked evilly. Then noticing the X under my ear, his expression turned devilish. "Oh, now that is quite interesting, isn't it?" He seemed amused at my pain. "Sweet on a Fugitive, are we?" He pulled out a gun, "I'm sorry, but it's for the greater good of the society. Shame, really." I thought of my mother at his words, the solemn look in her eyes, the muddy gray of her cloud.

I squeezed my eyes shut, gasping from the pain, and waiting for it just to end. But instead of hearing a gunshot as I had anticipated, I was knocked out of the Sentinel's grip. I quickly scrambled to the ground and searched around for the Sentinel's gun. Was I dead? I was supposed to be dead. But instead, I saw Griffin crouching in front of me.

"Aw, you're sweet on me?" He asked, giving me a wink and helping me up. The Sentinel lay on the floor a few feet away, blood spilling from a cut on his temple.

"Whatever," I let out a breath of relief, I wasn't going to die. The pain in my arm wasn't as bad now that the Sentinel wasn't digging into it, but everything still sounded like I was underwater on my right side. Refocusing on the task at hand, I scanned the mayhem around us. There were so many Assassins, too many. We were outnumbered. Why were they in the Opulent towns? Weren't they just Outsider gangs? Where was the advantage? How could we win? Then I saw it. The head building shining at the center of the Opulent town.

"Griffin, I know what I have to do," I said, locking my eyes on the building.

He followed my gaze, unsure. "You're going to get yourself killed."

"Hey, if I wasn't killed by the most wanted Fugitive to ever live, I think I'll be fine," I smirked, picking up a broken piece of wood laying on the floor, wincing a little at the strain on my arm.

"You flatter me," he rolled his eyes, "but if that's your weapon choice, you must be insane." Then seeming to get an idea, he pulled out a jet-black dagger. "This is the dagger that got me through all those years, Tess. Make sure you bring it back and make sure you come with it."

"I will." I took the dagger in my hands, taking in its silver detailing.

"Don't make promises you can't keep," he whispered with a small smile curving his lips.

"I'm not, Griff. And Sugar didn't either." I put my hand on his shoulder, quickly checking that no one was around us.

He smiled, "I adored her, Tess, and I…feel similarly towards you."

"Maybe if I make it back alive, you can elaborate on that." I smiled, offering him a quick kiss on the cheek, and running off.

Chapter Twenty-Five

It was possibly even dumber than our first plan, but it made sense. Without a leader, they were defenseless, and I had a feeling it wasn't going to be too difficult to take on the Head Official. It was still a long ways away, and I hoped I wasn't too late.

Avoiding all of the Sentinels stalking around the city wasn't an easy task, but thankfully they were stretched thin and I managed to sneak by most. The others that I wasn't so lucky around was where the dagger came in handy.

The head building was quite possibly the tallest in the entire nation. Our flag was blowing in front, a navy blue rectangle with the symbols of all five of the ranks arranged in a star. The immaculate walls were a light creme color, at least thirty feet tall, and held more windows than all of the houses in the Standard sector combined. Its tall poles seemed to touch the sky, and its lush lawns were *too* perfect. I didn't like how easy it was to get in. No guards, no defenses. This was wrong, nothing this important should be this easy. I walked along the grand halls; they resembled the type of luxury you'd expect to see in a palace. Gold pillars and paintings that looked like they cost millions lined the walls and staircases. I approached an elevator and knew that if I wanted to speak with the best of the best I'd have to go to the very top floor. It was a long way up, and the music was terrible, making me glad that I couldn't hold on to the tune. I was happy that I had the song that I did, not only did it lead me to Griffin, but at least it was catchy.

Finally, the elevator doors opened to reveal a glass floor beneath me. I nearly screamed when I looked down. It looked like I was going to fall through the clear glass to my death hundreds of feet below. A huge garden the size of a football field filled with flowers and stone benches could be seen beneath me. It would have been nice under different circumstances.

I approached a large set of oak doors and wondered if I should knock. This was where the major broadcasts were filmed...huh. I pushed open the door to find an empty room except for one chair and a big control panel. I had no idea how he hadn't heard the door open, but it had to be him. Sitting on what resembled a throne was a short and chubby man who wore a mink robe and a crown. Mr. Rafael Lieu, the man behind it all. He was looking out the huge glass windows with a smirk on his face, and the cloud over his head was a muddy shade of yellow. This was going to be easier than I thought. Approaching quietly, I raised the dagger, ready to strike at any moment.

"I wouldn't do that if I were you." He said, turning to face me. He waved his hand at the knife as if all this was putting him out. He wore a content expression as if no one could hurt him. "Hmm, let me guess." He flipped through a massive book by his side. "No, no don't tell me!" He giggled as if this was all just a game to him.

"Ah, here we go." He squinted at me as if inspecting me. "Blonde, blue eyes, 5', Standard… Here it is! Tethys, is it?" He looked back at his book. "You're not Hyperion, right?"

I gulped, hearing his name again. "No."

"And I trust you know who I am?" He smirked, looking amused.

"Of course I do," I rolled my eyes. "You're Mr. Lieu, descending from Henri la Beaulieu himself."

He looked satisfied, then as his eyes wandered to the X, he gasped. "Oh no, my dear! What have you done? What did he do to you?" He sounded concerned, like he actually cared for me. "I remember your drawings in school! You were our best student." He crossed his arms over his bulging belly. "So much potential…yet, used so easily." He gave a grim nod, and spoke softly, "did he hurt you, sweet child? Did it hurt to be used for something that rightfully belonged to you all along?"

I blinked, beginning to ask myself, then quickly shook my head. "O–of course not!"

"Manipulation is a powerful thing, isn't it?" He mused, giving me a pitiful look. "May I ask, was it worth it?"

"I–" Stammering, I tried to push his words out of my head, but they were so convincing, so sincere. "Stop it, you're nothing but a coward."

He chuckled, the exact kind of laugh I had imagined him to have. "Name-calling, are we? I suppose it would only make sense for you to repeat what he did to you." He shook his head, giving me the same condescending look. "I'm quite sorry, if I had known what he would do to you, I would have made sure he died five years ago." *What did he mean?*

"Five years ago?" I felt my grip on the dagger slacken a little, I hadn't meant to let go.

"At the war, my dear." He explained patiently. "Did he not tell you?"

I remembered the book entry and smiled a little. "Kind of."

"Quite interesting," he gave me a humorless smile and gently patted the chair across from him. I stood my ground not wanting to be trapped there. "I understand you do not trust me, dear, but I am only doing what's best for you, as I am for the nation."

I stared into his gentle eyes, and for a second considered believing him.

"If I recall correctly, he was the one who took your own mother's life, was he not?"

"How'd you—"

He cut me off, waving his hand in dismissal. "Don't you think I'd find out if one of my lovely citizens had been killed by the very Fugitive that we are after?" He shook his head grimly, as if the very thought made him sad beyond belief. "You're not an accomplice, my sweet girl. It's not too late to do the right thing. You can join us, the people who helped your family prosper for years! You can aid us in rebuilding Lieu, so no one is unhappy."

Words failed me as I considered what he was suggesting. I could go back to the way things were before they had died. I could have a normal life and get *them* back. I'd have the possibility of getting married, and even starting a family of my own. I could have everything I had ever dreamed of as a child, everything I ever knew to be true would fall back into place. There'd be no uncertainty, which I seemed to be drowning in these days. Yet, I'd have to betray everyone who had given so much to get me here. Sugar, Mary…Griffin. Oh gosh, Griffin. I'd have to leave him behind; I'd have to turn him in to be *killed*. All those Outsiders and Standards, they'd die. But what if I *could* make it better? What if this was the peaceful solution I had been searching and asking for all along?

"I have one condition." I started, trying out this new approach. "The rebels and Griffin all live."

He sighed, shaking his head, "My dear child, I have no problems with the Standards who were tricked into this horrible concept of revolution living. Even the Outsiders as deceitful as they were! They are simply thieves who couldn't see the powerful manipulation through the pain of their starving, and suffering." He gently took my hand, looking at me like a father comforting his scared child would. "But I am afraid I cannot let him live. Mr. Chainbreaker has committed far too many crimes against Lieu, including the murder of the very people you are vowing to protect. He belongs with all of the other Fugitives, dead and forgotten."

"But..." I was at a loss for words. So much fighting prevented, so many lives saved for the price of one. From an outside view, the choice was obvious, simple even. But picturing a life without him, I just...I couldn't.

"Tethys, I understand that you have developed some form of feelings for Mr. Chainbreaker, but I cannot let him drag you in this far just to hurt you, or anyone else for that matter." He added, taking my hands in his once more. "I can assure you that whatever Stockholm syndrome you have established towards him, he does not return."

"Y–you're lying...he," I stopped myself, realizing he had never actually said it. I couldn't justify him at all. Didn't he love me? A voice in the back of my head whispered, "*What if he was using you?*"

"Am I?" He asked innocently. "Maybe, you are lying to yourself, it seems you have a hard time telling when someone is lying."

I opened my mouth to speak but quickly shut it again, biting my lip. He was right...how was I to know if he was lying and not Griffin? *Stop it! He's just trying to confuse you.*

"It's problems like these that the ranks stop from occurring." He sounded so sincere. So reassuring. I believed him. I didn't want to believe him. "You could be with a lovely Standard right now, one that can actually say he loves you. One that is not just using you for what you can give him."

Frustration settled in me, and I raised the dagger again. *His dagger.* "I don't believe you."

His eyes betrayed him as the true fear showed for a second, "I–I wouldn't do that if I were you. I have people–"

"You talk too much," I said pushing past him towards the control buttons.

"What are you going to do with that?" He asked, laughing.

"This." I pressed a bright button that matched the description that they had given me and saw my face looking back at me. It worked.

"No don't–"

"Citizens of Lieu, my friends, family, and people. Our leaders have been lying to us, they kill for no reason as you have seen. I stand here with the man behind it all, who just sent people to kill all of the innocent Outsiders. People with less than us, yet kinder than we could ever be. Nothing he does is for us, it's all for him. So stand up, we're taking back what should have been ours all along. I have your leader, Sentinels, you have lost. Surrender now or face the consequences.

"Love is so many things, it's wonderful, it's confusing, it's magical! Not something you can force people into. It just happens! Don't you want to choose? Insiders! Don't you want to have the freedom to be songless, and feel good about it? They've made so many mistakes, and just blame them on you. And it's time we fought back. It's time we did something for once, actually questioned them for once! This is the start of a new era. One with freedom, and real solutions. I am not the leader, and neither is this guy. For once you are in charge of yourselves. Sincerely the Rebels." I pressed the end button, feeling accomplished. The entirety of Lieu had heard that broadcast, and there was nothing that Mr. Mink robe could do about it.

"That wasn't very wise, my dear," he said, the anger clear in his tone. "That wasn't very wise at all."

"You don't have a voice anymore," I snapped, but the look in his eyes made me fall back a little. "They're done answering to you."

"Oh?" He smiled evilly, and before I could move to stop him, Sentinels flooded into the room. "I gave you a chance for a better life, *Tess*." He spit the word, a deadly fire in his eyes. "It's a shame you didn't take it."

I screamed as they pulled me away roughly. I was sure I was going to pass out from the wound in my arm. I didn't know where they were taking me, and all I could do was watch his smug expression as he fled from the room.

Chapter Twenty-Six

My screams were useless as they took me down hallway after hallway; they didn't care. No one in this place cared. I just hoped that my broadcast helped him. That it eased the Assassins and Sentinels he was dealing with. Unless I was too slow…and–no! I wasn't going to let that be a possibility in my mind.

The Head Official's words rang in my head. Why did he have to make such perfect sense, and how did he know so much about us? Had he been watching us? I shuddered at the thought.

"Walk." One of the Sentinels commanded, snapping me out of my thoughts. I stopped struggling, knowing that it was just a waste of my energy. Instead of leading me down the entrance halls I had used before, they led me down further into the depths of the building. The garden that had seemed so far away before was now right beside me as they took me down winding, dark corridors.

Finally, they stopped in front of a small cell, with rusty bars and a flickering lightbulb overhead. It looked as if it had been abandoned for years.

"In," a woman, who looked around my mother's age barked, "and if I were you, I wouldn't attempt to escape." Her lips curled into a cruel twisted smile. "If the motion sensors think you are trying, you will be electrocuted."

"Won't that kill me?" I asked, panic bubbling inside me.

"Of course not," the first sentinel laughed. "Mr. Lieu wants that pleasure for himself."

I watched them walk away laughing, considering what they meant by that. Was I going to be executed? I curled my knees to my chest and hugged them. The past few days had all been too much to handle, I had lost everything, everyone I ever loved, and I had no idea how they were doing out there. Was Griffin dead? Had we already lost? I felt so useless. Was I ever going to see if they succeeded? Were they going to kill me before I even had the chance?

I sat there in the dusty cell until the light ran itself out, engulfing me in darkness. I felt so overwhelmed, and alone. Is this what true hopelessness felt like? Like you're just a ghost in your own body, waiting for it to be over. I thought of Griffin, understanding him a lot more. I wanted a way out, I wanted it to be over. I was tired, so very tired. When I eventually cried, I thought it would be sobs that wracked my entire body, not the silent, gentle tears trickling down my cheeks now. How had I gotten here? Why wasn't I at home with my dad, Hyperion, and my mom? Why had he left? Why had he died? Why had he killed her?

Bitterly I looked down at the cold, dirty floor. This was my final chapter, this was how it was ending. Would anyone remember me when I was gone? Would anyone grieve my death? Or would I just be another cloud gone dark?

Chapter Twenty-Seven

Voices stirred me from my sleep. "Should we wake her?" a familiar sounding voice asked.

"She might put up more of a fight," another voice echoed. I drowsily opened my eyes to a male and a female Sentinel, one of which had a bloody bandage covering one of his temples. I smirked as I recognized the Sentinel who always seemed to walk us to our deaths. First my brother, and now me. Maybe it really did run in the family.

I pushed myself onto my elbows, sitting up. "Where am I going?" I tried to sound confident, but I couldn't hold back the fear that crept into my voice.

The Sentinel I had grown to know, gave me a humorless smile. "Trust me, you'll know very soon." I let my eyes wander to his name tag and smirked. Diego. What a lovely name for such a horrible person. He grabbed my injured arm roughly, seeming to take pleasure in my quiet whimpers. I was terrified and felt so very alone. Where were all those Standards and Outsiders that *I* had put here? If we lost thousands today it would be my fault. I didn't know if it was selfish or not, but even though there were far more lives on the line all I could think of was Griffin. Would he survive? Was he already dead? I didn't know, making me feel even more helpless.

I was led into a room far grander than I would have expected for a prisoner, it looked more like a room fit for a king.

The female Sentinel instructed me to sit down, before leaving with Diego. I heard the door click shut and lock, confusing me further. I was left alone for a few minutes before the door opened to three timid looking maids. Outsiders taken into service by the looks of their calloused hands. The three ladies split up, one entering a massive wardrobe, and the other two walking into a grand bathroom. I noticed that all of their clouds were a dreary shade of blue.

"Hello?" I stood up, peeking into the bathroom after them. "What's going on?"

"Mr. Lieu wants us to prepare you." One of them, her name tag read Charlotte, patiently explained. I tilted my head to hear better, everything still sounded muffled on one side.

"Prepare me for what?" My heart skipped a beat, as a few ideas came to mind.

"The broadcast," Charlotte gave me a sympathetic smile.

The first maid walked out of the closet, holding three torn dresses. "Come with me, miss." Her name tag read Camila.

I hesitated, "What is the broadcast for."

Camila, pulling out a measuring tape, didn't meet my gaze. "Surely they told her." She whispered to Charlotte. I didn't know what she was talking about.

"Of course they didn't, Camila." The third maid pointed out, holding an assortment of supplies in her worn hands.

"Do they just expect her to figure it out, Aria?" Camila gave her a pointed look, before beginning to measure around my waist.

Aria shrugged, "I figured she got the message after the cell."

"What's happening?" I threw my hands out, frustrated. I was tired of being left in the dark assuming the worst.

"You are going to be executed today, miss," Charlotte said gently, beginning to brush my hair.

"So what's all this about?" I asked, trying to stop myself from thinking about it.

"If you ask me, I think Mr. Lieu is trying to send a message to everyone," Camila whispered, beginning to stitch a delicate treble clef to the middle of the dirty dress.

"What do you mean?" I asked, fear surging through me.

Aria gave her a stern look, "You'll only worry her. It's fine, miss."

"This isn't a coincidence, Aria," Camila mumbled, stitching a jagged black X over the treble clef. I noticed that the dress had a cut that exposed my upper back lacing around the back of my neck. I didn't like how symbolic all of this seemed to be.

"It seems today that he is reminding all of Lieu that no matter what rank you are, you cannot overcome the Officials," Charlotte whispered, tears coming to her eyes. "I thought things could change, I really did."

"You were a part of the rebellion?" I blinked, taking her in.

"Not directly, but…I had hope." She looked at me with admiration. "You gave us hope, something we haven't had in a while."

I was touched, honored to have been such an impact on Lieu, yet ashamed that all of that was for nothing.

"I'm sorry that it didn't work," I mumbled, looking down. "What's the X and treble clef for?" I asked, trying to change the subject.

"They symbolize how you were a Standard and then the Fugitive destroyed that beautiful symbol," Camila explained, giving me a pitiful look.

"'The Fugitive,' is named Griffin." I crossed my arms, feeling defensive. Griffin hadn't trapped me at all, the ranks had.

"All the same, I'm very sorry." Aria gently pulled half of my hair back with a ribbon.

"For what?" I looked back at her, unsure.

"For having to go through that of course. The songs are a very intimate thing, and that was taken away from you." Aria set her hand on my shoulder, giving it a small squeeze.

"It wasn't," I looked down. "It was made better." I could feel myself smiling and aching for him more than ever. When I died, I would have never heard how he felt, but I held comfort in the fact that he would have no doubt of how I felt.

A sudden question came to my mind, "Who are the Assassins working for?"

Charlotte looked taken aback. "Mr. Lieu, why?"

"No reason," I mumbled, understanding a lot more now. So that's why they showed up so fast today.

They all remained silent as they finished me up, putting on the torn, dirty dress. It was the color of our flag, but the deep blue was stained with dark red splatters. A cool breeze coursed up my exposed back, making me shiver. I looked at myself in the mirror, almost not recognizing the bruised, scared face looking back at me. I wasn't that little Standard girl anymore, she'd died when Hyperion had. I couldn't save her.

Chapter Twenty-Eight

I shivered as they led me behind the huge stage. On the platform were five tall wooden beams towering over me in the shape of a star. A bucket sat beside one of the poles with metal rods sticking out of it. Steam billowed into the air, dark gray hues drifting across the stage. On either side of each beam was a rusty iron cuff.

Mr. Lieu's voice came without warning, echoing across the entire city. "Greetings my lovely citizens, ranked big and small! Today I have before me the foolish rebels who tried to stop Lieu, but they forgot one small detail. Lieu does not lose!" Cheers —from the Opulents most likely— erupted around the front of the stage.

"Rebels watching before me from your pathetic seats, you are powerless against this nation, and you have betrayed us. You all know how we handle traitors. But in my mercy, I have spared you! You owe me your lives today, the lives of thousands! Long live Lieu!"

The crowd chanted after him, and the cameras were catching every word. "Come forth loyal servants, pay the debts of the thousands around us. No one is stronger than us, no one can overcome us! Leader of the rebels, traitor of Lieu, come forth. Watch as we take away from you what you have taken from us." I couldn't see anything, but I was sure he meant Griffin. My heart skipped a beat, he was alive.

"These rules have ensured peace for hundreds of years! Let us recite them and learn one new rule that has been added as a permanent reminder to all.

1. *Never consult with an Outsider*

2. *Never break curfew*

3. *Never steal from someone above your rank or someone that shares it*

4. *Never harm someone from the same rank or higher*

5. *Insiders are extremely dangerous mistakes*

6. *Always keep your eyes open for the brand*

7. *Never, under any circumstances, deny a Sentinel or Official*

8. *The government always knows what's best for you*

9. *Never associate yourself with someone in the lower ranks*

10. *Sentinels have every right to ask and search to prove your innocence*

11. *All Insiders will be killed on sight*

12. All Outsiders now have an earlier curfew of 7:30 P.M. anyone caught outside after this will be shot on sight

13. Any citizen, no matter the rank, who consults or aids a Fugitive or Insider will be stripped of their rank and marked as a traitor and enemy of Lieu

14. Once a month a family from every rank will give up one child as payment for the sins committed today

I covered my mouth with my hand, unable to believe what he had just declared. *A child? An innocent to be sacrificed for what?* How many families would lose their main provider in desperation of not losing their little ones?

"Rule fourteen will serve as a reminder of what happens when you go against Lieu, and just how powerless you have all become because of the events today." He raised his hands and as if they had been given some unseen cue, I was led onto the stage. "Today will be remembered for years to come! My faithful citizens, be thankful that only five die today. Only five lives are given today for the price of millions!"

I looked across the crowd of cheering Opulents and Standards. A sea of bright clouds. How could these people cheer for the deaths of innocents? Outsiders stood watching at the foot of the stage, all bearing shackles and chains. Where were the Standards that had joined us? Of course he had forgiven them without any punishment. Their punishment was a whole new kind of torture. They were about to witness just how cruel Lieu could be.

Chapter Twenty-Nine

As I was pushed onto the stage, I saw Griffin. His feet were bound together with heavyweights, and a metal chain pulled on his neck, cutting into it, binding him to the heavy post behind him. They pushed me towards the place where Mr. Lieu sat, forcing me onto my hands and knees.

"My sovereign." I began, reciting the lines they had drilled into me. "I will pay for my crimes today before you and our nation, with my life." I bit my lip to stop myself from screaming at him.

He gave me a small nod, unable to contain the smug look on his face. "Go forth, my servant, pay your debts." I was forced to my feet once more and turned to face the poles.

Griffin's desperate eyes were locked on me as the Sentinels forced me towards the beam beside the tallest, center pole. They pushed me onto my knees with my exposed back facing the crowd, and secured my wrists in the cuffs.

The roaring crowd was so loud, that I couldn't hear anything but the blood pounding in my ears. I strained my neck, trying to see him around the pole. He was pulling against the chain causing it to dig in deeper, screaming out for me. Tears came to my eyes as I watched him. I tried to call out to him, but it was useless, he'd never hear me over the crowd, and I was going to die.

Mr. Lieu silenced the crowd looking smug, and Diego stepped forward, about to deliver another Cliffblazer to their death.

"My dear nation, I come to you as one of you. Just a soul trying to serve their beloved homeland." Diego began, walking across the stage over to me. "I have before me a Standard just like you, who thought she was above the law. She has broken countless laws, one of which involved aiding a Fugitive and even daring to form an intimate bond with him. She stands before us today as a traitor of Lieu, you have no home here anymore! You will be treated as the one you so love, a Fugitive!" He screamed, ripping one of the rods out of the bucket, sending hot steam around me. "Tethys Victoria Cliffblazer, as punishment for your many crimes you are hereby stripped of your rank and will be branded as the Fugitive you have so clearly become! Mr. Lieu with his thirst for justice will put an end to your treason today for good! Long live Lieu!"

The crowd chanted after him even louder this time, but all I could do was look at the beam in front of me. There was no warning that could have been given for the pain I experienced next. Hot metal pressed into my flesh, causing me to let out a blood-curdling scream. My eyes filled with tears as the pain deepened and I cried out again, begging for it to end. I was dying…I was dying. The world was going dark around me, through the cheering I heard screams and a sickening crack. I watched through my tears as Griffin was whipped, struggling harder against the chains binding him. This was a whole new kind of torture; I couldn't move.

"Griffin," my voice sounded funny and came out as a feeble and hoarse whisper. "I love you," I croaked aching to close my eyes. I wanted it to stop, everything was too loud, too bright. I had to get to him. I couldn't move. I couldn't save him.

"I love you, Tess! I love you so much!" Griffin's voice cracked from the strain, as the Sentinels whipped him across his chest this time. He loved me. We were going to die. There was no more time. I needed more time.

"Take me!" He screeched clawing against the chains, blood seeping down his face from the whip mark. "Take me instead!" He let out another blood-curdling cry as they whipped him again, but all of it sounded miles away. I was so tired. So very tired. "Tethys, hold on!" His words were piercing through the crowd less and less, and just as the excruciating pain became too much to bear, I was roughly pulled to my feet by the Sentinel.

"This Standard now bears a new brand! A symbol for her cruel actions against Lieu." Diego locked me securely to the beam so that I was facing the audience, supported by the heavy chains. "The treble clef signifies what you once were, and the X signifies what you have become. May this brand be engraved in your flesh even in death!" The crowd's cheers were lost in the muffled screams of the Outsiders. "You have betrayed Lieu; you have betrayed Henri la Beaulieu himself! You will die as a warning to millions of Standards after you. *This* is what happens when you try to overpower the great nation that we have fought for years to protect!" The Opulents were going crazy, cheering, and even throwing flowers at his feet.

Smirking, he walked past me to the beam on my right. The highest point of the star. "I have here before me an

Opulent citizen who thought their rank put them beside Mr. Lieu himself. Even the highest rank, even the strongest cannot overcome the founders!" More cheering erupted as a terrified looking Opulent child walked across the stage. His cloud was a violent shade of purple, the cloud that Drew had worn like a brand.

This was a little kid, how heartless were these people? They were cheering for his death just as they had for Sugar. The poor little boy had a streak of paint across his face, no doubt from the revolution. "No one is above the law! No child, man, or woman. No Opulent, Standard, Fugitive, or Outsider can ever defy the foundations of our great society! Come forth sinful servant, pay your debts to the nation of Lieu."

The little Opulent boy wordlessly walked over to the Head Official, his bottom lip quivering. "My sovereign," his high voice was shaky, and he sounded as if he was on the verge of tears. "I will p–pay…for my crimes today before you, and our nation, w–with my life." He whimpered as hot tears began rolling down his cheeks. I was surprised he even got through his lines.

"Go forth, my child, pay your debts," Mr. Lieu nodded his head and the Sentinels ripped him away and secured him to the center post.

"Timothy Theo Mercier, you have broken the sacred rules that hold our nation together by consulting with the rebel forces and conspiring against us. You are a disgrace to your family and have committed treason to this nation. As punishment for your crimes, you are hereby sentenced with the death penalty! Long live Lieu!" Diego raised his fist in the air, roaring with the crowd as they chanted it back. I watched as Timothy broke down again, crying out for his family. I wished I could save him. I could've saved him.

Diego walked to the empty post beside me, seeming particularly excited. "As you all know, Insiders have been an issue for years. Wreaking havoc and killing the lives of innocents such as yourselves." I gritted my teeth. *What a liar.*

"If I had to thank the rebellion for one thing, it is that some of these wretches made the mistake of revealing themselves." With a deadly look in his eyes, I watched in horror as Miss García was led onto the platform. She didn't look scared, instead, she held her head up high as she crossed the stage towards the Head Official.

"My sovereign," she began getting onto her knees, smirking. "I will pay for my crimes today before you and our nation, with my life."

He nodded, seeming taken aback at her confidence. "Go forth, servant, pay your debts."

As she was led over to the post beside me, she gave me a little wink taking me by surprise. What did she know that I didn't? Was she just happy to die? It didn't seem likely.

Diego, disregarding her smirk, stood before the crowd once more. "García Hernández Pérez, you have hidden from us for many years. Lying, and conspiring with the rebel forces. You stand here today a traitor and a stain on our society. The only punishment fit for you is the death penalty! Today you claim the shame you have brought upon us!" I watched her calm expression in confusion.

The Outsider that had wired the explosives stepped forward onto the stage as he began. "The Outsiders have always carried the price of their crimes on their backs, but it seems that not even the Assassins are enough anymore." He smirked as the hunched over man made his way across the stage to Mr. Lieu.

"My sovereign," he began, his deep voice steady and calm. "I will pay for my crimes today before you and our nation, with my life."

"Go forth, humble servant, pay your debts." Mr. Lieu seemed more and more unsettled by their calm natures. He glanced around, seeming to check for any sneak attacks.

The man walked over to the pole on the other side of Timothy, waving away the Sentinels. They firmly chained him down, seeming angered by his casualness.

"Liam Charleston Hill, you have aided the rebels in the destruction of numerous monuments. Including the very stage, we once used to record our broadcasts on." His voice had a sense of authority as it rang across the crowd. "You will pay for these crimes today with your life, serving as a reminder for others of just how gracious we've been with your kind for far too long.

"And finally, we have quite possibly the most severe display of treason in all of history."

Walking to the post that Griffin was bound to, Diego gave him an evil grin as if he had been aching to do this for a while. "Griffin James Chainbreaker, your sins against Lieu are by far the greatest we have ever seen! You have postponed your punishments for these offenses ever since you were sixteen years old! You have murdered, and maimed hundreds, including the death of both your father and a Standard woman."

"She was going to kill her!" Griffin roared, struggling against the chains trying to reach the Sentinel.

"And now you are the reason that she dies today!" The Sentinel cried, his voice ringing over the sound of his screams. Griffin let out a loud groan as he was slashed again, silencing him.

Diego went on, "You have put countless lives in danger, and have been living with these crimes weighing over you for over five years. You are the reason that these citizens die today and every month from this point on." His voice rang louder than it had before, and it was filled with an angry passion. "You have killed those you love most, and you watch them die today because of your actions. There isn't a penalty severe enough for your crimes, Griffin. I can only hope the shame and guilt are enough to torture you more than we can." He turned to face the crowd again, raising his fists in the air. "You will be struck thirteen times for the thirteen years you escaped the wrath of this nation on the brand that you have worn since you were thirteen years old! Then you will be killed, just as you have done to so many others. May your crimes haunt you long past death!" The crowd exploded into cheers louder than ever before; they had been waiting for Griffin to die since the day he had been discovered.

Chapter Thirty

Diego and the other Sentinels surged forward unchaining Griffin and ripping the shirt right off of his back, revealing the brand to everyone in the audience and the entire nation watching.

Then taking out a long whip from a bucket of water, called out to the crowd. "One!" Griffin groaned, his back tensing as he curved into the beam clawing against it. I screamed out for him, starting to move but quickly stopping when the pain became blinding.

"Two!" This time he screamed, a sound that I hoped I would never hear again. My vision was turning black at the edges from my agony, but I needed to stay awake. I needed to help him. I pulled against the heavy chains, feeling like my limbs were turning to jelly. With each strike, his cloud grew fainter.

"Three!" The sickening sound he made snapped me back into it, and I tugged again but to no avail.

"Four!" Sweat dripped down his forehead from the exertion as he clung onto the beam.

"Griffin!" I called out to him, my voice still sounding hoarse and choked up. "You're almost there! It'll be okay." I hoped that he could hear me, even if it was faint. "We're going to make it, remember? No matter what." He lifted his tired eyes up at me, grimacing.

"Five!" He screamed again, scraping his hands down the beam. I watched, helpless, as the crimson blood dripped menacingly down the post. Staining his once white hands, and turning them into a nightmarish shade of red. With the way his breathing sounded, I was worried he would pass out. I didn't feel much better myself.

As they raised the whip for the sixth strike, a loud shout echoed across the square. Diego turned, letting the whip fall at his feet.

"What is this?" Mr. Lieu jumped to his feet, screaming at the Sentinels. "Why did you stop?"

I couldn't believe my eyes. Storming across the Opulent town, Mary and hundreds of people with dirt coated, worn clothes marched raising their fists in the air.

"Vive la révolution!" They screamed, hoisting their varied weapons in the air. I watched as the order fell into chaos. Opulent citizens were screaming, rushing out of their seats, the Outsiders bound by chains were cheering, raising their fists high into the air despite the weight of their shackles. Mr. Lieu was trying to soothe the crowd, but his voice was drowned out by the rebels. He was overpowered. They outnumbered the Assassins, who were gawking at the mismatched group. They pushed through their forces surging towards the stage. Miss García began unchaining herself using a bobby pin, and it suddenly made sense. All of the confident glances, the winks. They had known. They had known this was going to happen.

Once she had freed herself, she hurried over to me, trying to break my own. I watched as Liam freed the little Opulent boy, and a rush of adrenaline coursed through me. We hadn't lost at all earlier today, our victory had only been delayed and was now being broadcast for all of Lieu to see!

"Can you walk?" She asked, finally unlocking it. I nodded my head, trying my best to control my breathing as I made the slow journey over to the place where Griffin was bound. His head hung at a concerning angle as he coughed up blood, his breathing sharp and jagged.

"Hey," I dropped to my knees beside him. "Hey, Griffin, it's going to be okay. You just need to hold on for a little longer." I tried not to focus on how faint his cloud had become. The wisps of smoke above his head resembled what Hyperion had worn right before he died.

He looked up at me, tears welling in his eyes. "I…I don't know how much longer I can hold on." He wheezed again, crimson blood sprinkling the post.

I frantically began trying to get the silver shackles off, "Griff, we have to move, your mom is here."

He nodded struggling to his feet beside me. I looped my arm securely around his shoulders trying to steady him. He let out a sharp cry of anguish as he took another step forward.

"It's okay," I slowed down, helping him stumble forward. He nodded, and I continued steadily leading him across the platform, sweat trickling down my forehead.

I watched as the battle unfolded, Outsiders and Sentinels clashing. It was pandemonium, hundreds of clouds all coming together. Every color I could imagine.

Mr. Lieu stood at the front of the platform, too deep in shock to move. I turned in his direction, a determined fire boiling within me. This was the man that had taken Drew, my brother, Sugar, and so many others. This was the man that had controlled me my whole life, had *trapped* me my whole life. This man had driven countless people to live in unbearable fear, sent so many innocents to their deaths. I would never live another second in peace until his blood stained the pavement of the town I had grown to hate.

"Almost there," I grunted in between pants. Griffin gave me a grim nod, stumbling forward, his breathing staggered.

"Rafael Lieu!" Mary's voice rang across the platform as she rose up past the crowd. "Killer of millions, captor of thousands! You stand here today no better than the very thing you swore to destroy: a Fugitive! A murderer with no motive except for his thirst for power! There is no punishment worthy of the crimes of you and your ancestors." She reached him, nothing but hate in her cold eyes. "You killed my daughter, and today you try to kill my son. It will never be enough for you; there is not enough blood in the world to quench your thirst!"

"Vive la révolution!" The crowd roared, saluting. I saluted with the Outsiders, thrusting my fist high into the air.

"You have destroyed the very virtues that you swore to protect," she continued, forcing him to his feet. "You declared war while you preached peace! You promised happiness and prosperity while the lower ranks starved! There is no speech, no sacrifice that can pay for the pain you have caused us. This nation has neglected the needs of its people ever since Henri la Beaulieu, the man you called a savior!

The very thing you swore to protect is now the result of your downfall. May these crimes haunt you long past death!"

He looked around at the people, tears filling his grey eyes. I could see the desperation in his gaze as he scanned the crowd. The Assassins had been defeated; the Sentinels all gone. He was alone, and no one would weep when he died.

Chapter Thirty-One

"Do you deny these accusations, Mr. Lieu?" Mary asked, gracefully stepping around him to face the crowd.

"I…" He froze, terror crossing his face. "It was for the good of this nation!"

Mary scoffed, turning on him. "Today you will die for the pain you have caused this land. You will mark the end of a reign of terror and the beginning of a new era!"

"You will destroy what we have fought for years to protect!" He screamed, desperately turning to face the crowd.

"I think you've done a plenty good job of that." She snapped, then facing me, her expression softened. "Tethys, my dear child, I think you should be the one to do this."

I gulped and gave her a grim nod before completing the journey to where they stood. Mary gently took Griffin from my grip, stepping aside.

I looked across the group of people, if I hadn't gone through all that I had, I would likely be standing among them today. We were giving them a future, one I had thought impossible, yet today we took the first step towards it.

"I come before you as not your leader, but as one of you." Tears came to my eyes, and I blinked them away. We were finally going to break the system that had once been declared unbreakable. "I grew up thinking there was no chance of change, and that we had no need for one. I grew up watching my loved ones perish and blaming it on everyone except the real cause. The society itself. Our system was corrupt, but no one could even get a glimpse of that because all we saw was what we were told to. We've been guided on a tight leash for our whole lives, and I don't want that for my children. For your children!" I looked around at the young members of the audience. "This isn't mercy! Forcing young kids to die for the sins of others isn't justice. Rules that restrict our every thought isn't a form of peace."

I walked over to the center post, picking up the shackles. "Whether you can see these chains or not, doesn't mean they aren't restricting you. We have been forced into ranks, divided when we are so much stronger together! Torn apart so that we could never overthrow our oppressors." I walked over to the post bearing the mark of the Insiders. "Dear people, persecuting innocents for the sole purpose of being different isn't protection, it's murder. Driving people to steal to stay afloat, because you gave your resources to those who had more than enough, then punishing them on the same degree as murder isn't justice. It's cowardice. It's neglect." Walking back to the front of the stage, a newfound determination coursed through me. "Lieu is not a wonderful nation, it's not a place with full of customs to celebrate. It's a vile land, built on a foundation of corrupt, unjust laws. But today we begin the long process of changing that. Today we initiate the first steps of a new nation. One that stands together, where these lines that have been engraved into our minds so deeply will be erased!" I forced Mr. Lieu onto his knees, feeling no remorse for what was about to happen. "Vive la révolution!" I screamed with the crowd, taking in my hands the very gun that had ended my mother's life.

Mr. Lieu met my gaze, a blank expression on his face as I pressed the gun barrel to his forehead. "You can kill me," he whispered, his voice so quiet that I barely heard him. "But this moment will forever be etched in the darkest corners of your mind. I will always be there when you close your eyes. When you let your wildest fears wander, you will see my face. Tethys Victoria Cliffblazer, you can kill me, but through you, I will never truly die."

I stared into his cold eyes, speechless. *But you will die,* I thought, pressing the dark metal to his forehead firmly once more. *And so will the ranks that have divided us for so long with you.* I looked over to the place where Griffin and Mary stood, his tired gaze meeting mine. He gave me a grim nod, and that was all I needed as I turned to face him again. The sound of the gunshot was lost in the deafening cheers of the crowd.

Epilogue

Five Years Later

As the years flew by, the colors faded. With every passing season, I noticed them less and less, seeing the people behind the clouds. I saw the light and the dark mixing together to create the people surrounding me. A little of each because no one was just one. A lesson that I had learned over my lifetime.

The audience could be heard applauding as the broadcast ended with the ruler of Britain shaking hands with our newly made president, Mary. The Fissure War had officially ended after many attempts with not only Britain, but also with our previous allies in France. These efforts had saved the thousands of lives that had been trapped in the horrid boot camps Mr. Lieu had put into effect, 'training' them to fight. Griffin had told me a few stories of his time in the boot camps, and none of them were good.

I clapped along with the crowd even though they could not hear me through the screen. The cameras panned across the varied audience, making a wide grin spread across my face. I still found it strange to see the Outsiders standing beside the Opulents, even though the ranks had finally been erased completely, along with all of the Chanteuses' songs. The children who had been left with songs before this would find their soulmates as usual, but it would be a choice whether they got married or not. I had high hopes for the way our nation was forming under the rule of Mary. Justice was already being served, and peace was being well maintained. She had secured most of our old allies once more and had formed many new ones. This land was going to prosper, and I was only sad that I wouldn't get to see it.

The Outsiders and Insiders had been pardoned by Mary and declared citizens of the young nation of Liberté, but Griffin was a different story. We could not simply pardon all that he had done, seeing how murder was still murder no matter who ruled, so Mary 'accidentally' let him slip past the law forces leaving us standing on the outskirts of Liberté.

"Are you scared?" He asked, smiling down at me, and slipping the silver ring onto my finger.

I met his warm gaze and shook my head. "No, not anymore." I grinned down at the gleaming metal, before helping him slip his own on. "Are you?"

"No," he laughed, looking across the wide expanse of land before us. Great big plains as far as the eye could see, rolling hills covered with bright grass. It was breathtaking.

The wind billowed around us, whipping our hair and clothes. This was it. This was where a new chapter began. So many were lost in the previous story, so many lives gone who would never get to see this, but I would. I would see it all for them. Sugar, Drew, Hyperion, my dad…and my mom. I would spend each day treasuring the things they never got to, leaving the clouds where they belonged: in the past.

Griff smiled as he took in the view, his green eyes twinkling. He turned back to me and took my hand in his own, "Ready for whatever comes next?"

"Ready for whatever comes next."

Acknowledgments

Before I get to all of the other thank-you's, I'd especially like to acknowledge all of the lovely readers! You guys rock! Like seriously guys, I could not have done this without you. So, thank you! *fist bump* Ok now, get to bed if you stayed up late reading this!

Next, a big thank you to my sister Haley, for listening to my rants about Colors at midnight, helping me make the story better, and being a better artist than me.

To Mrs. Been, my eighth-grade creative writing teacher, thank you for inspiring me to venture deeper into storytelling and improving upon my ideas. You continue to be an inspiration in my life as I continue writing, practicing all you taught me, so thank you! *hugs*

To my super awesome BFF Elizabeth, thank you for sharing my enthusiasm, helping me edit, expanding my ideas making the story so much more interesting, and just being overall an amazing person! *air hug* I could not have eliminated all those extra commas without you!

Dad, thanks for not shutting off the Wi-fi, and helping me set up all of the technical stuff! *high fives*

Mom, thanks for helping me create the cover of this book, and with this whole process! You helped me design a cover more amazing than anything I could ever dream of, and I cannot thank you enough! You have always encouraged me to follow my dreams, and none of this would have been possible without you! Thank you for helping me accomplish something I thought to be impossible before, I love you!

And above all, I would like to thank God for giving us the ability to form such complex ideas and putting this creativity in my head. Without His ingenious creation of words, I'd be lost.

Thank you.

The Fugitive's Tale

Stay tuned to the next installment in this series coming soon!

Prologue

I had only been eight. The smoke had already been black. My dad started like we all did, happy, and just trying to get by. Then it all changed.

He started coming home late at night angry, with no time for anyone but himself. I could always smell the drink on his breath, see the change in his eyes when he walked through the door. The smoke turned from crimson to black over the years. The color as dull as our lives.

My brother was dead, and he had been for six years now. His death had taken many things from us, and my mother's joyful spirit was no exception.

My three younger siblings couldn't see the smoke. I was the only one, and no one believed me. No one except my mother. She had always listened; she didn't give me the looks that the others did. Those sympathetic looks.

I didn't have time for sympathy, it was a waste of hope. A childish thought that anything would ever get better. I knew it wouldn't. I knew that Bullet wasn't coming back. I knew dad would never feel the pain that his death had brought on to us. After all, a murderer never mourns their victim…

Printed in Great Britain
by Amazon